WHERE THEY GRAZE WITHOUT FLOWERS

A NOVEL BY

R. JOSEPH

i

Library of Congress Control Number:2019909509

Editing J. Zebley V

First printing, 2019.

ISBN EBook   978-1-7339892-2-0
ISBN Print   978-1-7339892-0-6

www.wheretheygraze.com

In Memory of Roberta
The greatest storyteller I have ever known

To Wendi
My Light

Table of Contents

Foreword:
Where They Graze Without Flowers

By Steve Edington

When Jack Kerouac wrote *On the Road* he offered his readers a series of overlapping landscapes: There was the geographical landscape of the America of the late 1940s immediately following the Second World War. There was the interior landscape of the novel's two principal characters, Sal and Dean, as they pursued there sometimes frantic search for what Kerouac called "joy, kicks, and darkness" as they made their way back and forth across Post-War America. And then there was spiritual landscape of America itself in that Post-War era, a country seeking to return to "normalcy" after WWII even as there was an undercurrent of restlessness and furtiveness on the part of many of those coming of age at that time. The key line in that book, as I read it, is the one that asks, "Whither goest thou America in your shiny new car in the night?" Which is to say: Where are you going, America, with your new gadgets and gizmos, along with the wealth and power you've come to attain?

So, it is hardly a coincidence that Kerouac surfaces from time to time in R. Joseph's *Where They* Graze *Without Flowers*. To be sure, it's his own novel, told in his own captivating style, and with the spirit of Kerouac hanging around.

Joseph, too, offers us a series of landscapes. The geographical landscapes will take you from Texas to Louisiana to Chicago to Mexico to England and Scotland, and to the Maryland and Delaware shores. The time span is from the mid-1950s to the mid-1970s. As you move across these landscapes of time and place you will encounter the interior landscapes of a wide ranging cast of characters—each of them engaged in their searches for meaning and purposes in their lives, both on their own and when their lives intersect. Each of them, in his or her own way, is on a religious and spiritual journey.

One of my friends and colleagues in the Unitarian Universalist ministry, the late Rev. Forrest Church, defined religion as "Our human response to the dual reality of being alive and knowing that we will die." The people you'll encounter in the pages ahead are each living out this understanding of religion; they are seeking what it is that brings value and spiritual depth to the lives they are living in the face of their mortality.

There is Rev. Kin whose ministries take him from a small church in East Texas to a prison chaplaincy in Maryland, with various other stops along the way— including a time in England. And all the while he ponders on the true essence of the God he seeks to serve, without ever fully knowing finding it.

There's Sal. And I do not take it as a coincidence that R. Joseph gives one of his principal characters the same name that Kerouac gives his persona in *On the Road*. Sal's spiritual journey takes him from running a bar in Chicago to living the life of a writer/poet in Mexico and gaining a measure of fame as a spiritual guide/guru.

There's Caroline who finds herself a childless widow when her husband is killed attempting to avenge the death of their daughter. Her spiritual travels are those of picking up the pieces of a broken life and seeking to move on.

There are numerous others who take their interior landscapes across the physical landscape of this novel. I'm guessing that somewhere in these varied, and yet related, lives the reader will find some of his or her own. If you look deeply enough into them you may well find some of the life you live as well.

The underlying metaphor R. Joseph gives his readers here is that of ripples. For me they bring to mind some lines from a poem by the late Rev. Ric Masten—the one-time poet laureate of Carmel, California. They read:

A pebble does not enter a pond
Without creating ripples
That in turn
Reach many shores.

As you read this book, I suggest you think of yourselves a one of the many shores that Ric writes of. The ripples R. Joseph creates are both the characters you find as well as the story his narrator, who checks in from time to time, tells.

The ripples metaphor meshes well with that of yet another character named Boat. It's not until you get to the end of the novel that you fully learn the role Boat has in the various stores it contains. [And, hey, no peeking ahead!] It is R. Joseph's invoking of ripples and his character of Boat calls forth these beautiful lines by the late, and much beloved, Pete Seeger:

Somos el barco, somos el mar.
Yo navego en ti, tu navegas en mi.
We are the boat, we are the sea.
I sail in you, you sail in me.

Sail on, dear reader, sail on!

Rev. Steve Edington is the Minister Emeritus of the Unitarian Universalist Church of Nashua, New Hampshire. He is the author of **The Beat Face of God; Bring Your Own God—The Spirituality of Woody Guthrie;** *and* **God Is Not God's Name—A Journey Beyond Words.**

grat·i·tude

/ˈgradəˌt(y)oōd/

noun

the quality of being thankful; readiness to show appreciation for and to return kindness.

Sarah, Phil, Jane, Jim, Victoria, and Jake. Thank you for the generosity of your talents and time. Your reviews and suggestions were essential, and are appreciated.

Steve, for your inspiration and support.

J. Zebley V, for your editing recommendations.

Michael Mclaughlin, adding your voice.

To my friends who have engaged, humored and endured me.

WHERE THEY GRAZE WITHOUT FLOWERS

Ripples

I watch as his boat drifts into the sunset. Muted hues of red and purple that have escaped from behind the horizon find temporary spaces in the sky. Thin brushstrokes of gold and orange glow along the horizon and paint the undersides of low-hanging clouds. The setting sun throws out a last beam of soft, glimmering light over the water and directly to me. The boat is now a silhouette against the sunset.

I hate goodbyes.

As I watch his boat fade into the darkness, I feel the wind grow colder and stronger. Small waves begin to lap below the dock. Not ready to let go of the day, I zip up my jacket and sit cross-legged at the edge of the dock. A lone light buzzes and illuminates above me.

I scoot forward and let my legs hang over the edge of the dock. Leaning forward, I watch the water become still in between cycles of small waves. All the usual analogies of life - the calm and the turbulent - come to me as I watch.

Looking around, I notice a handful of scattered small stones on the dock near me. *I'm sure the things he said were true*, I think as I stretch to gather the stones in my reach.

I lean over the dock and drop one of the small stones into the calm water below and watch as ripples slowly push out from the center. As the ripples fan out, a new cycle of waves come. I watch the waves until they slowly recede. When the water again becomes still, I drop another stone into the water.

His words are still in my mind. Ripples within ripples are stories within stories. There is no beginning. This is where the ripples start, only to give themselves back to the water, from whence they came.

The Mission

A small church sat alone against a barren landscape of honey mesquite trees, Indian grass, brown dirt, and pale blue sky. The church, made small against the landscape, was a long forgotten Spanish Mission.

The paint that hadn't peeled away from the Mission's exterior was white. Behind the peeling paint, the wood was gray. A small steeple leaned slightly to one side and cradled a bell that hadn't rung in decades.

Each side of the Mission held three rectangular windows with large, fixed panes flanked by narrower panes. At the front, steps climbed from the ground to a small landing. At the top of the landing, weathered, double doors opened to the sanctuary. A small window sat to the right of the double doors and faced east. Scorched by the sun, the Mission barely had a pulse.

It was Wednesday afternoon. Beads of sweat ran down Reverend Kin's forehead as sat at his desk, working on next week's sermon. He squinted against the sunlight that shone through the dusty front window

4

over his desk. Drops of sweat fell on his page as he wrote, waiting for his appointment.

His given name was Paul Sage. He became known as Kin by telling folks, when he first arrived, that they were all truly kin. Over the years, the kidding of it fell away, and he was, in fact, Reverend Kin to those who were both as hard and dry as the land on which they lived.

Against the noise of the wind, Kin heard an approaching truck echo through the Deep East Texas valley. He stood, looked through the dusty window, squinted, and held his hands above his eyes to see a blue Dodge pickup racing over the dirt road that led to the Mission. The pickup was followed by a trail of dust that slowly rose and resembled the tail of a dragon against the cloudless sky. *Tribulation and dust,* he thought.

Kin took a last sip of coffee and put his cigarette out in the ashtray. He blew smoke from his mouth and nose. He snapped his collar on over his button up black shirt, brushed off his jeans and made his way towards the confessional that sat at the back of the Mission. He stopped. "Son of a bitch," he muttered and went back to his desk to retrieve his Bible. He walked across the planked floor to the confessional, holding the Bible in his left hand.

He opened the door on the far side of the confessional and took his seat. The only noises were the sounds of the wind, the sound of the approaching truck, and his breathing. He closed his eyes and leaned his head against the side wall of the confessional.

The narrow confessional was refurbished at the request of those in the congregation who felt the need to confess, to repent. The words *Confession of evil works is the first beginning of good work,* by Saint Augustine were hand painted on both sides of the inside dividing wall. Cowboys, mothers, farmers, Mexicans, Indians and Gringos confessed their sins, their desires, their fears and darkest secrets through a hammered tin plate with punched holes.

Soft pockets of light pushed through the cedar plank walls of the confessional and found Kin. The colors that surrounded him were greys, muted browns, off whites and shades of black.

Kin listened as the Dodge skidded to a stop in front of the Mission. He could hear the dust blow against the same window that had bathed him in filtered sunlight. Even though he had taken confession hundreds of times, his heart started to race.

Sitting in his Dodge, Lee Pratt was dehydrated from the wind, the sun, and his tears. Dust swirled around his truck as he tried to collect himself. He didn't notice the wind or the dust and barely remembered driving to the Mission.

Lee was the only son to parents whose family had a large ranch and raised cattle in Jasper for three generations. He had a wife, Caroline, and a seven-year-old daughter named Annie. Caroline was a mix of Native American Indian, Mexican, and Gringo. She started working on the ranch in her late twenties and never left, falling in love with, and marrying, Lee.

Lee leaned over and opened the glove box door. With shaky hand, he reached in and grabbed his pistol, a Smith and Wesson. Leaning over on his seat, he gripped the wood handle and spun the cylinder to make sure it was fully loaded. He sat back up, leaving the glove box door open, and held the gun in his lap. He reached out and unlatched the driver's door. The door opened slightly. Lee sat still, took a deep breath, and then another.

After a few moments, he quickly pushed the truck door open with his foot, stood up, and put the gun inside his waistband, against the small of his back. He pulled down on the side of his shirt, making sure it covered the gun. Lee climbed the wood steps to the landing, and stood like a statue in front of the weathered, double doors as the wind blew against his back.

Suddenly, he turned and walked back down the steps to the passenger side of the truck. He reached around to his back, grabbed the gun from his waistband, leaned in through the open window and placed it back into the glove box. He slammed the glove box door shut. As he stood straight, Lee looked around the barren landscape to make sure no one was watching him, something only done by a man who rarely carried a gun.

From inside the confessional, Kin listened as Lee climbed back up the steps. He heard the Mission doors swing open.

Lee entered the Mission of Christ Church, bringing the wind, the dust, and his tribulation. He walked heavily across the wood-planked floor to the confessional. His footsteps echoed across the empty room and sunlight followed him through the opened doors to the angled shadows at the back of the church.

As he listened, Kin tried to let go of expectations. He knew why Lee was there. He knew of the incident between Lee's family and the Tent Preacher.

Kin's mind flashed to the Tent Preacher who was not an actual Preacher, or Reverend, or Minister. He thought of the Tent Preacher's traveling Gospel and Healing Ministry and their tent revivals. In his mind's eye, he could still see the sign in front of the tent that read, *Come to Expect a Miracle.*

Kin had urged his congregation not to attend the traveling Gospel shows. "To those of you who struggle, to those of you who feel desperate, do not put your faith into, or receive your faith from a traveling carnival. The Lord seeks faith and consistency. The Lord desires you to be steadfast," he preached from his pulpit. "I understand the temptation," he empathized.

Lee and Caroline did not go for themselves. Sadly, Annie had become sicker and weaker. After a series of x-rays, medicines and therapies, Lee and Caroline were told by Annie's doctor to consider prayer and ask God for a miracle.

The Gospel and Healing Ministry held tent revivals for six straight nights in Jasper. Each night Lee, Caroline, and Annie walked by the sign that read *Come to Expect a Miracle.* Each night they put money in the basket. Each night they listened to the Tent Preacher's words. "You have to believe with all you have." And each night, people claimed to be healed.

On the last night the revival was in Jasper, the Tent Preacher walked to Annie, looked at Lee and Caroline, and laid his hands on Annie's head and shoulder. She looked up. The lights from the bulbs strung in the tent illuminated the Tent Preacher. She watched the Tent Preacher. He looked to the sky and screamed to the heavens as if they were his very own, speaking in words known and unknown. She saw his face turn red and the veins in his temples stick out. She felt strangers reach over and touch her while gospel music echoed and blended with all the sounds. To Annie, everything seemed to come from the Tent Preacher. She thought he was an angel. She believed him.

The Tent Preacher stopped. Exhausted and covered in sweat, he looked to Lee. "In God's name, your daughter is healed." He said it with all the confidence one could speak. The crowd exploded in cheers and praise. Lee and Caroline hugged Annie and embraced each other.

Everyone who witnessed, believed. People cried out, "I love you," and "Amen," and "Glory Be," and "Thank you Jesus." People were moved to their core and lives were changed on the spot. Many who had traversed long distances traveled back with incredible stories of hope and healings. inspired to live better lives for themselves. After all, they were there to expect a miracle, just as the sign had said.

The tent revival rolled out of town. Six weeks later, Annie died.

Every man has a breaking point, and every man responds differently to tragedy. Some die inside, some find purpose, and some do both.

And from that, two men were seated in a poorly lit confessional, lost in thought and separated by a thin piece of punched tin. They sat in silence for a long time. Lee leaned close to the tin. His elbows were on his knees and his hands were clasped. "I've known you a long time, Kin," he said in a low hoarse voice, "and I respect you."

Kin said nothing.

Words pushed through the punched holes of tin like a mist of sorrow. "I've lost my daughter. I've half lost my wife," Lee moaned. Then, his words shot through the tin like bullets of their own. "I'm going to kill a man." It wasn't what Lee said in as much as how he said it.

"You still have a choice," Kin replied, knowing whom Lee wanted to kill.

Lee responded without emotion. "I'm not here to be saved -"

"Do you think this will be easy?" Kin cut in. His chair scraped the floor as he instinctively moved closer to the punched tin, his fingers clenched together.

"Bury me next to my daughter," Lee responded flatly. "I expect no quarter." His words ensured finality.

Kin heard Lee's chair slide back as he rose to leave. "Sit down, Lee," he said. "You have a wife who loves you, who needs you. You have people who care about you. You still have a life to be lived."

Lee said nothing.

Kin started again. "We've known each other a long time. You know I've seen a lot, we both have." He leaned back from the dividing wall and sighed. "Being a spiritual person, a forgiving person is hard, harder than killing a man." He paused and made his own confession. "Do you think I wouldn't have the same thoughts if I was in your shoes?"

There was no response. Kin waited. Lee started to sob. He could barely be heard over the sound of the wind and swirling dust that blew against the mission. "I am here," Kin whispered.

After what seemed like an eternity, Lee asked, "Are you in my shoes?"

Kin cleared his throat and responded, "No Lee."

Not satisfied, Lee raised his voice. "Are you in my shoes?" he asked, almost screaming.

"No, I'm not in your shoes," Kin said. He repeated his words louder to calm Lee. "No, I am not in your shoes, Lee." His words filled the empty mission.

"No, the hell you're not," Lee responded, lowering his voice.

After more silence, Kin attempted to give final direction. "Go back to your family, Lee. Be loyal to your faith. Be a strong man."

"I was loyal to my faith," Lee replied defiantly. "I don't need to live like this, without my Annie. Who says I got to go on like this?"

Kin paused and searched for an answer that made sense to him, much less to Lee.

"That man," Lee started and then paused, "cannot say those things in God's name." He tried to speak more, but his voice broke as he worked to control his grief.

Before Kin could reply, the door from the other side of the confessional opened and slammed against the wall. Footsteps echoed across the floor and out of the Mission. Kin heard Lee's feet pound down the steps and the door to his Dodge open and slam shut.

Kin turned his chair, leaned back against the wall and closed his eyes. His silent prayer started with the words "Take this with your hands."

The windows in the truck rattled when Lee slammed the driver's door shut. He turned the key, and the motor sputtered to a start. He opened the glove box, grabbed the gun and placed it on the seat against his hip.

In front of the gas gauge, a slightly curled picture of Annie sat against the beveled glass. With care, Lee pulled the picture back to make sure he had enough gas for the drive. He brought the picture to his face and tenderly kissed the image of his daughter. He held his lips still against the image for a moment. "Daddy loves you," he breathed out and placed the image of his daughter back against the instrument panel.

As the truck roughly idled, Lee rested his head on his hands that gripped the steering wheel. "This is something I need to do," he repeated to himself over and over. "This is something I need to do." His uncontrolled words and thoughts circled him like the swirling dust and dirt that blew against his truck.

Lee raised his head, wiped his eyes with his forearm, and pulled away from the Mission.

The Tent Preacher's traveling Gospel and Healing Ministry had moved on to Lake Charles, Louisiana, a three-hour drive from Jasper Texas.

At the same time, Lee pulled away from the Mission, Jason Watts - the Tent Preacher - lay awake in a cheap hotel room outside of Lake Charles.

Heavy curtains were drawn tight against the big hotel room window. Only random sharp streams of light cut through the darkness of the room, enough to illuminate the cigarette smoke that lingered in the air, an opened suitcase and scattered clothes on the floor. Half-empty glasses and bottles sat on a dresser. Across the room, country music pushed out of an old AM radio. A woman he had met the day before was asleep next to him.

Lying on his back, he watched as cigarette smoke floated through the streams of light. He strained his eyes, trying to make out shapes from the cracks in the ceiling. Giving up on sleep, he turned on his side and watched her as she slept. His eyes followed her dark hair. He noticed how it fell across her face and over her tanned shoulders.

Exquisite, he thought to himself and gently brushed loose strands of hair away from her face with his finger. He took a breath and carefully pulled himself up to a sitting position. Trying not to disturb her, he reached for his matches and cigarettes on the nightstand. He lit a cigarette, took a drag, exhaled smoke, and watched her again as she slept in the heat.

Not wanting to sit still any longer, he slowly pushed the sheet off his legs, lifted himself out of the bed, and walked through the drifting smoke and sharp streams of light. He found an empty glass on the dresser, poured two fingers of scotch and mixed in flat Ginger Ale left from the night. "Sweet Mamie Taylor," he sang to himself. Jason turned towards the sleeping girl, raised his drink in the air and whispered, "And to you, my sweet little Angel, a silent toast."

At that moment, she woke up gently, sleepy and smiling. "Hey baby," she said as she stretched.

"Well now, hey you," he said and walked to the bed. Jason sat his drink on the nightstand and dropped next to her. He put his face close to hers, playfully kissed her on the cheek and rubbed his nose against hers. "Morning Sugar," he said in a slow, rehearsed southern drawl.

She smelled the scotch on his breath, paused, pulled her head back and soberly scanned the room. She saw the mess and smelled the stale air. "This place looks different than it did last night. It smells in here. You need to open a window. And why, why do you always call me Sugar?" She sat up in the bed and scooted back against the headboard, pulling the sheet up to her neck despite the heat. "Did you forget my name already?"

He scooted up to her, ignoring her question, "You know Sugar, I've been meaning to ask. How old are you?"

She gave him a blank look, leaned over, and grabbed her watch from the small nightstand on her side of the bed. She squinted to make out the time. "Dammit," she said looking at her watch, "Don't you worry. I'm old enough, and you promised me breakfast." She held her watch up to him. "And it's almost three in the afternoon. How are we going to get breakfast now?" She pouted as she said it, tossed her watch back to the nightstand, and slumped down in the bed. "And you got your thing tonight and I'm hungry as hell Jace."

He sighed, picked up his drink, finished it in a single swallow, let out a growl, leaned over and wrapped his arms around her. He put his mouth close to her ear and whispered. "Well, that's right Sugar, you gonna come on down and see me? I'll put you right up front and you can tell 'em all I saved you." He pulled his head back and looked at her, waiting for a sweet response.

"No," she said, pouting like a little girl, "and I just got to say, you ain't no kind of ordinary preacher."

He lifted himself out of the bed and walked back through the dark to pour another drink. Standing in his boxers, he grabbed the bottle of Scotch. "Want some, Sugar?"

"No," she said as she watched splinters of light reflect from the bottle of Scotch as he poured his drink. "You drink a lot?" she asked.

He walked back to the bed, placed his drink on the nightstand, and sat beside her. "Well Sugar, you are right. I'm no ordinary preacher. The way I see it, there ain't no sense in being an ordinary anything, not in this life anyway."

She turned over on her stomach and rested on her elbows Without saying a word.

"No one should want to be an ordinary anything," he continued, leaning over and trying to catch a reaction. "You know what I'm saying Sugar?" he whispered, running his fingers through her hair.

"No, I just feel hungry" she said, still pouting. "Do you know what I'm saying?"

He smiled and gave a slight laugh. "Now Sugar, don't be like that," he whispered.

"Like what?" she asked.

"Being angry, just being an ordinary person doing ordinary things, like getting mad." He sat back down next to her. "Now listen here, Sugar. I saw it early, being ordinary and sad. Dust storms chased my Momma and Dad out of Oklahoma. The old man never got over it. He got beat." His voice picked up, his words came quick. "Doom and gloom, doom and gloom, over and over, doom and gloom."

"That's absolutely terrible," she blurted out.

He continued speaking without noticing her reaction. "Family farm near Stillwater lost. And, all the way across to California, doom and gloom and crying. Half time I'd have to hustle for food. You don't understand what it's like to have a beaten man as your Pop."

"Maybe," she said.

"Yeah, maybe," he replied, "well, that's when I made my decision."

"Decision?" she asked.

He took a sip of his drink and placed it back on the nightstand. "I don't know when, you know, I was a kid and all. But I decided I would not give in, no how, no way, no matter what," he explained.

She moved closer and put her head on his leg. "But they lost everything. What about your mother?"

He looked down at her. Her eyes were closed. "Now, Sugar," he said in a soft easy tone, "you can gain and lose everything a hundred times in this life. I loved my momma and I'm sure she's just fine."

"You left your parents?" she cried out, opened her eyes, and shot up to a sitting position.

"I told you I made a decision," he replied. "I would not grow into a beaten man." He looked across the room as he spoke. "I stayed a few years and then I left."

"Without a word?" she asked.

"I left a note," he answered.

"A note?" she gasped, leaning back against the headboard, folding her arms across her chest. "Just a note, have you been back?"

"No," he answered without a trace of emotion.

She started to talk and then stopped. She thought for a second, squinted her eyes and then asked, "What did you do then?"

Jason grabbed his drink from his nightstand. "I did what I did, odd jobs, hoboing. I slept everywhere." He smiled at his memories and took a sip of his drink. "I slept in boxcars, in tents, on benches. I worked with horses, on trains, circus work, all of it." He reached over and grabbed his Bible. "Then, this here Bible saved me. You see, not only did it give me hope, I use it to give others hope. See, no doom and gloom here Sugar."

"Well, do you think God likes what you did?" she asked right away.

"Who knows, Sugar," he replied. "Maybe one day I'll tip the scales." He gave her a quick kiss. "I like to think that if I'm broke, I'm perfectly broke."

"Well, if confidence accounts for anything, you'll be fine," she concluded. "But," she added, "You are handsome."

Lost in his own thoughts, he never heard what she said. "Now listen here, Sugar," he called out, "can you tell me with one-hundred percent certainty what the truth is anyway?"

"No, but, "she stammered.

"I knew you'd say that," he shot back, "cause no man can. And even those who preach and read this here Bible can't agree on it anyhow." He tapped on the Bible, leaned over and whispered words perfumed in Scotch. "Sugar, I'm not in the truth business. I'm in the hope business. They can all go find their own damn truth."

She said nothing and blew air from her mouth to rid her of the smell of Scotch.

Without warning, Jason jumped to his feet. He downed his drink and wildly flipped through pages of his Bible. His lips moved as he silently read passages. He stopped and looked at her. A smile grew big across his face.

"What?" she asked, sensing his excitement.

He tossed the Bible on the bed. "Now look, look over here, Sugar," he called out, jumping across the room. "Lookey over here now, Sugar!"

She laughed as he bounced across the dark room to the large draped hotel room window. "You are a crazy man, Jace," she yelled.

Jason, the Tent Preacher, stood at the window, his voice rose as it did under the tent. "Sugar, I am not the light. I am the man who pulls the shades back to show you the light!"

With that, he hastily pulled open the heavy curtains. Light flooded the hotel room like a burst dam, filling every empty space with Louisiana sunlight. She ducked under her covers, laughing. "Close those curtains, you crazy, man!" She screamed out.

He stood at the window in his boxers, looking out at a dirt parking lot, lonely highway, and barren field. "This is something I need to do," he repeated to himself over and over. "This is something I need to do."

Caroline's Moon

1953 - Jasper, Texas

Lee Pratt was never able to face his daughter's condition. His thoughts were swells of abstract answers and resolutions that were wrapped in hope. His mind lived in a place where things were better.

It was Caroline who was present with Annie, who held her at night and who told her the story of the Moon.

Caroline believed the Moon to be, kind, loving, and easy to forgive. "Moon has been through so much and has seen even more," she would tell Annie. It was her way to remind them both that they were not alone, that the Moon would somehow see them through. Caroline told Annie the story of the Moon as it slowly rose through the sky, as they waited for sleep.

Caroline whispered slowly and clearly, "There was a time when the Moon was sad when she wept for ages. The Moon felt empty, alone and helpless." She spoke in a soft voice as she imagined the Moon would, "No one cares about me. I am alone and trapped. It's dark and the stars are so far away."

Caroline gave Annie a gentle squeeze. Her voice changed as she switched to the narrator. "Each day the Moon silently pleaded for comfort. Moon's prayers went deep into the universe and past the stars. Each day that her prayers went unanswered, Moon became sadder."

Annie hung on every word as her mother continued. "The Sun never spoke, but without words he continued to shine his light onto the Moon. He was a loyal Sun," she informed her daughter with a smile.

Caroline looked down at her daughter, whose eyes were heavy. She spoke softly. "After ages of feeling alone and rejected, Moon screamed out to the Sun as they shared a pre-dawn sky."

"I am no thief," Caroline said with emotion as the Moon, slightly raising her voice. "I never asked for your light, Sun."

Annie opened her eyes and gasped. Her eyes locked with her mother's.

Caroline's voice lowered an octave. "This is true Moon," she said solemnly as if she was the Sun.

"But the Moon wasn't done," Caroline said excitedly. "She was so sad and hurt and lonely." Switching back and speaking as the Moon she went on. "I never hear from you or anyone to show me you care as I drift, alone and scared."

22

Caroline's expression moved from sad to serious. "The Sun did not respond," she said. Caroline was animated. Annie was captivated.

"Not satisfied," Caroline's voice rose, "the Moon, demanded freedom and screamed to the Sun. I never asked to be a thief of borrowed light!"

She paused and then whispered. "And the Moon just stopped." Caroline looked at her daughter with an open mouth and wide eyes, as to ask, *what will happen next?* Annie gazed back at her mother, waiting.

Caroline waited a full moment and then spoke, calm and steady. "The Moon realized her anger was only her own. It was hard, but the Moon told the Sun her true feelings."

Her voice shifted back as the Moon. "I'm sad and scared and I feel alone," she said tenderly, sharing her own true feelings through her story.

She gave Annie another gentle squeeze and continued. "The Sun never said a word. Moon fell below the horizon and sunlight filled the sky."

Mother pulled back to get a good look at her daughter's face. She studied her expression. She felt the closeness between them. Caroline smiled and her voice picked up. "When the Sun and the Moon again shared the sky, the Sun spoke lovingly." She touched the tip of her daughter's nose with her finger and continued. "I need you Moon," she said as the Sun, as a mother who needed her daughter.

Caroline took a breath and confessed, as the Moon, "But my light does not shine, it's your light."

Her eyes watered, her voice lowered, and she responded as the Sun. "It is your light Moon. It becomes yours."

Annie knew the ending of the story and mouthed the words she knew with her mother. "Just as the fish swim in the ocean and the trees and mountains are rooted to the ground, your job is to shine your light into the darkness, where it is needed the most."

Years later, Kin held back his own tears as Caroline recited the story of the Moon.

Come to Expect a Miracle

While Lee Pratt raced to confront the Tent Preacher, over 300 people were getting ready or on their way to the Gospel and Healing Ministry's tent revival.

It was stifling hot. Laborers, who had finished raising the tent sweat as they carried in chairs, speakers, lights and a podium. A man set up a popcorn cart near the tent's entrance and volunteers from the local church marked out parking areas in a neighboring field. The grass was sparse and knee-high.

Outside the entrance of the tent, Jason helped a group of men dig two holes that were four feet apart. They slid in two posts that were attached to a freshly painted sign. The sign was five feet long, three feet high and sat perfectly at eye level when in the ground. They painted the wood bright white with hand painted, black, script letters and gold shadowing that read, *Come to Expect a Miracle*. A spotlight aimed at the sign illuminated the message.

Jason stood back to inspect the sign. "You know fellas," he exclaimed to the men now surrounding him, "Women walk into our tent holding onto their hats

25

against the wind. The wind is like their fear. They feel hopeful as they walk by this here sign, men do too. You see, people want more than to just survive. Even if they don't know exactly what they want, or how to say it, they know they need something more than how they're living and how they're feeling." Jason stopped and pointed to the tent entrance. "This is where they find what they need." He paused and looked them all over. "You're doing a good thing fellas, thank you."

As the men responded, Jason grabbed the arm of the revival's manager and pulled him to the side as he started to walk. "Now listen here, you keep that basket moving," he said and walked ahead to greet volunteers that had just arrived.

Time sluggishly and defiantly moved forward. As the sun slowly descended, an early evening wind kicked up dust, enough dust to cover the tent like a thin coating of funeral ash.

Come to Expect a Miracle. It's everything that's good. It's everything hopeful. It's all-powerful. It's inspiring. It's action. Yet still it's just five words painted on a piece of wood.

Jason directed the late arriving volunteers and headed back behind the tent to get prepared. He had a process that required more than a few shots and a few prayers. He walked back and forth in the field behind the tent with a bible in one hand and a flask in the other. He rehearsed the night in his mind, yelling out Bible verses in between shots of cheap liquor.

Back in Jasper, Kin had pushed any concerns he had for Lee out of his mind, reminding himself that Lee was in God's hands. He had no idea Lee was on his way to Lake Charles, becoming more erratic and more out of control the closer he got.

As Lee drove, his thoughts, continuously and obsessively, returned to killing the Tent Preacher. He played out scenario after scenario in his mind. He couldn't think of anything else, or even anything to live for, as he drove furiously past farms, fields, lakes, and small towns. His pistol was on the seat next to him.

Losing all sense of time and direction, Lee ended up out of gas on a gravel road. He screamed, pushed the door open, got out of the truck and placed his gun back between his jeans and lower back. He kicked the truck, kicked at the dirt, slammed his fists on the hood, cried out and cursed, but never said a thing to God. He never asked for strength or asked why. He rejected anything that would change his course. Lee refused to see God in anything.

The sun, as if it could watch no more, fell into the horizon, bleeding hot orange and pink that hung low in the sky.

As Lee cursed and kicked in frustration, an old flatbed pickup, returning farm laborers from the fields, bounced down the gravel dirt road towards him. Lee jumped in the middle of the road, waving his hands. The truck's headlights shone on a desperate man on a dirt road.

The flatbed, which was missing a muffler, stopped in a cloud of dust and shook from the rough idle of the engine. Lee walked up to the driver's side.

"How far up Lake Charles way?" Lee shouted over the noise of the flatbed.

The driver of the truck, a man with a large mustache and straw hat, yelled back, "About eight miles, bear left the whole way. You'll go through some splits." Looking Lee over he asked, "You need a ride? Jump on back with the boys. I can get you halfway there." The driver turned towards the passenger side, reached over and grabbed a beer, a Pearl. Turning back with the beer, he nodded for Lee to take it, holding it before him.

Lee jumped back and shook his head. *No*, he said to himself. Then Lee shouted, "No!" He pulled his pistol and screamed. "Get out of the truck. Get out of the truck!" He became immediately impatient and screamed louder. "Now, I said!" He nervously pointed the gun back and forth between the driver and the men on the back, who were standing up by the cab. "Now!" Lee shrieked and accidentally fired a shot that rang above the men standing in the back.

The three men standing on the flatbed reacted immediately, scrambling over piles of produce on the back of the truck. Hay flew and tools clanked as the men leapt off the flatbed and ran down the dirt road. The driver, scared for his life, dove across the driver's seat and slapped at the passenger door handle. The door popped open and his legs flew in the air as he fell to the ground headfirst. The truck, still in gear, jumped forward, shook, and stalled. The driver rolled onto his side, scrambled to his feet, and zigzagged down the lane in fear of being shot.

It would be forty minutes before the men reached a telephone to call the police and tell them a crazy man tried to kill them, stole their truck and was headed to Lake Charles.

Lee jumped in the truck, reached over, closed the passenger door, pulled his pistol out, and tossed it on the seat. He turned the key, slammed the gas pedal to the floor and popped the clutch. The motor revved, the truck lurched forward and tools and produce flew off the back of the flatbed. The tires spun out in the gravel and squealed as the truck jumped on the asphalt road, headed to Lake Charles.

At eighty miles an hour, he passed a sign that told him he was close. *Three Miles to a New Life,* the sign read. Lee kept his foot to the floor. Both the engine and Lee cursed and screamed over the roads to Lake Charles, Louisiana.

The revival was in full swing when Lee arrived. He parked the flatbed in the knee-high grass without being noticed. He got out of the truck, put the pistol against his lower back, and stormed towards the tent. He walked past the illuminated sign that read *Come to Expect a Miracle* without feeling a thing.

He walked into the tent under the strewn lights and through the crowd, the voices, and the music. Toward the front, the Tent Preacher had stepped back into the aisle from the crowd after commanding an evil spirit out of a local drunk.

Lee walked up the center aisle with intent. As he did, he reached around to his lower back and pulled out the Smith and Wesson from under his shirt.

The few in the crowd who saw Lee pull his gun screamed. They tried to push through others who were moving closer to the Tent Preacher. Screams of "gun" were mixed with screams of praise.

Lee walked up the aisle. The rush of thoughts and streams of emotion that had obsessively and compulsively controlled him, that demanded action, collided with the reality that surrounded him. The faces were real. He felt the heat from the strewn lights. He could smell the popcorn. He heard the voices and the music. In an instant, he recognized the feelings of hope and excitement around him, feelings he wanted to destroy.

Out of nowhere, he saw the Tent Preacher as someone who, although careless, wanted to help people. Even if only for a split second, he felt sympathy. Still, he needed the nameless Tent Preacher to know what he did, what happened to Annie, what had happened to Caroline.

Jason, the Tent Preacher, heard the commotion and turned to see Lee walking up the aisle towards him. Before he could process what was going on, they were face to face. The crowd tightened around them.

Noticing the gun in Lee's hand, the Tent Preacher took a half step back and smiled. "Please, let me help you brother?" he asked.

Lee said nothing.

Jason figured Lee to be a harmless and misguided soul who was only in need of attention. He smiled and raised his left hand into the air, clutching his bible. As he stood with the bible raised in the air, Jason held his right hand out to Lee, asking for the weapon with a gesture. The crowd converged, waiting to see a new kind of miracle.

"You don't remember me, do you?" Lee yelled, his face a tear-stained portrait of conflict.

"No, friend, tell me, when did we meet? What happened to you?" Jason replied.

The moment Lee realized the Tent Preacher did not recognize him, he had no sense of Lee's family, their pain and tragedy. The moment he realized Annie was not important enough for the Tent Preacher to remember, the sympathy Lee felt vanished immediately. Conflict left his face, and he pulled the trigger three times, shooting the Tent Preacher in the stomach at point blank range.

Jason doubled over from the shots and fell to the ground. The Bible fell from his hand and lay next to him as he bled and lost consciousness.

The seconds that followed were pure madness. Two others fired eight shots. Four people died; Jason, Lee Pratt, a local farmhand, Zane Cole and Margaret Lepps who sang in the choir and played the piano. A self-imagined cowboy who emptied his revolver shooting at Lee accidentally shot Zane and Margaret. The cowboy dropped his gun as soon as he saw that his bullets took down Zane and Margaret. He left during the commotion that ensued. Another man shot his pistol in the air. Two others fell and were injured from the panic of the crowd.

Under the lights of the tent, Jason, Lee, Zane and Margaret lay, close together and motionless on the dirt floor.

Few questions were asked, and no fingerprints were taken. The police attributed all the murders to Lee. They surmised that Lee, a man bent on disaster, brought the two guns found on the dirt floor.

The murders took place Wednesday night, and the news didn't reach Jasper until Friday. No one in Jasper was prepared for the story that portrayed Lee as a deranged man who killed three innocent people, one a preacher.

The Lake Charles newspaper interviewed Jason's friend from the previous night. Sugar's name was Tracy Jensen. She stated that she called him Jace, and he had proposed to her the night before. She would only agree to be interviewed if they put her picture in the paper. She made the front page.

Zane was buried at a local church in Lake Charles. Over two hundred and fifty people came to support his family, which had been in Lake Charles for generations.

Margaret's sister brought her body back to the family plot in a small town near Sabine Lake on the Texas-Louisiana border. There was no funeral service.

The Gospel and Healing Ministry, now without a preacher, pooled enough money together for a proper burial before they all moved on. Not knowing who he was, a local minister from Lake Charles gave Jason a powerful eulogy. Over five hundred people attended the outdoor service. Jason "Jace" Watts was buried a quarter mile from where he was killed. The small wood cross placed in the ground over his body read, Jason Watts - Doing God's Work - October 20, 1954.

Kin convinced the Lake Charles authorities to release Lee's body so he could be buried in his family plot. He did not tell them about Lee's daughter or try to explain why he did what he did. Lee's body was on its way back to Jasper while Kin had his grave dug next to his daughter's.

Kin got the word out that Lee would be laid to rest on Sunday evening and there would be no Sunday services. Late Saturday afternoon, Kin went to the cemetery and helped the gravedigger dig Lee's grave. Neither man said a word as they labored under the falling sun.

There were too many thoughts and feelings for Kin to settle on one way to feel. His thoughts were too large to move and too abstract to comprehend. They lived in the undercurrents of his consciousness, feelings he did not want to feel.

On Sunday evening, eleven people came to pay their respects to Lee. Unable to stand, Caroline sat in a chair next to Kin as he spoke. Knowing that those in attendance were Lee's truest friends, Kin read a Bible verse about forgiveness and another about redemption. He closed the Bible, held it against his leg, looked straight ahead and said, "Lee was a good man." He wanted to say something about life being hard and breaking points, but thought better. After a moment of silence, he finished. "I am sure God knows it all the more." Realizing that everyone was in too much shock to speak, he concluded, "Thank you for coming." Besides a few handshakes, no one said a thing and everyone left feeling numb.

At next Sunday's service, Kin preached on forgiveness, faith and persevering when one lacked faith. He wanted to be available to anyone who needed to talk. He wanted to be there. He encouraged his parishioners to come to him for counsel if they needed it.

No one did.

As Delicate as an Unbroken Thread

1955, Lake Rayburn, Texas

Being the wife of a murderer didn't come with much sympathy, even if you had lost your daughter. People in Jasper wanted to put the entire situation that happened in Lake Charles behind them. Unfortunately, that included Caroline.

Through the winter of 1954, Caroline Pratt spent most of her time looking out a small window. The small window was on the South-West corner of The Rayburn, a group home for the elderly and others who had difficulty living on their own. It was no accident that Caroline Pratt ended up at the Rayburn. Kin called in every favor and pulled every string he could, raising a few eyebrows in the process.

Caroline was quiet. "I have to concentrate to breathe," was how she described her state of being to Kin. "I feel as delicate as an unbroken thread," she confided.

Support from her family came in the way of weekly visits, in shifts. One week her parents would visit then her sister, and the next, her brother. Her brother and sister never brought their children to visit. They did not want them in *that kind* of place. Caroline met with a counselor each week and Kin visited every Wednesday at 2:00 PM.

Kin held onto the advice he received from an old, bearded minister when he asked, "What do you say to someone who has experienced tragedy? I can never find the right words."

"You say nothing," the bearded Minister advised. "You just need to be there."

With that knowledge, Kin was the only person not trying to get Caroline to open up. "Let things come to you," he encouraged.

Often they sat near a window and never said a word. Sometimes, they played chess and sometimes they read. When it was nice outside, they sat on a patio or walked through the Preserve that led to Lake Sam Rayburn.

Almost every night, Caroline watched the sun fall behind the expansive valley and a nearby hill. A hill that *had just lain down and take a nap*, she thought to herself. She watched wildlife of the area, always looking for her favorite, the Mourning dove.

Her room was sparse. Three of her own paintings hung on the walls. Cut flowers were in a vase whenever she could pick them and rocks, found during her walks, sat on her windowsill, her dresser and her desk.

Photographs of Lee and Annie sat in a drawer. She could not leave them out. When she felt exceptionally strong, she would set them out a few hours at a time. There were long spaces between those times.

Weeks rolled into months, winter turned into spring and by the summer of 1955, Caroline was taking longer walks along the lake. Sometimes she walked with Kin, usually she walked alone. She felt stronger and knew it was time to leave the safest place she had ever known.

"Do you know what I'll miss most?" Caroline asked late in the summer.

"Tell me," he replied.

"The little slate patio under the Loblolly Pines that overlooks the valley. I want a little patio under a grove of trees wherever I go," she said.

"So you're ready to go?" Kin asked.

"Yes," she responded.

Her improvement was not lost on her baby sister Ginny. For the first time since she visited, Ginny did not look at her watch every five minutes. For the first time, she brought Caroline flowers.

The two sisters sat under the sun at an old, wrought-iron table away from the house. Ginny spoke first as they pulled their chairs to the table. "So tell me, how are you?" she asked. She didn't wait for an answer. "You look so good Cissy."

Caroline took a second to make sure Ginny was ready for her reply. "I'm doing fine Virginia."

"Virginia," Ginny laughed. "You haven't called me Virginia in forever."

"About the same time you last called me Cissy," Caroline said. She looked past Ginny, out to the stand of Pines that threw shade on her favorite patio. "The breeze feels wonderful doesn't it?" she asked.

"Yes, it does," Ginny replied with little interest, looking back to see what Caroline was looking at.

"And how are you Ginny?" Caroline asked.

Ginny turned back towards Caroline. Her expression froze, and her face changed.

"Oh, Cissy. I can't tell you," she moaned. She bent her head down and put her face in her hands. "No one understands how hard things are for me." Her breathing became heavy, and she lifted her head up out of her hands. Her face was red. Her eyes were watery, and she rubbed them with her palms. "I didn't want to say anything, while you know," she hesitated, "while you were here." She looked at the ground before she spoke again. "You know, in your condition and all." Ginny paused, put her elbows on the table, and put her head back into her hands and started to cry.

Caroline reached across the small table and placed her hand on her sister's shoulder. "What's the matter, Ginny?" she asked. "I'm fine. You can tell me."

"Bobby left me," Ginny said. She sobbed with her head still in her hands. "He left me. He left the kids. He didn't even take his own damn kids, just left them all with me." Her tone moved from sorrow to bitter.

Caroline leaned in closer and reached to Ginny, gently stroking her hair. "I'm so sorry, Ginny. You can do this," she whispered.

"It's been three months," Ginny squealed from behind her hands.

Caroline pulled Ginny's hands to the table to see her. The wind blew Ginny's hair across her face. Her face was red and her eyes were dry.

"You don't know what it's like to just lose someone," Ginny blurted out.

Caroline said nothing.

Ginny continued. "The bills, my job, the kids. I have no time to myself." She started talking faster. "And, you know Dr. Johnston?"

"I do," Caroline replied.

"Well, he says if I don't find a way to relax I may–"she looked away from Caroline as she finished, "have a breakdown of sorts."

Caroline tried to calm Ginny. "Well, I don't think it's anything you can't–"

"No, it's true," Ginny cut Caroline off. "I can end up in bad shape." Caroline released Ginny's hands.

Ginny took a deep breath, reached up and pulled her hair back and out of her face. "Damn wind," she said, took another breath, smiled and reached across the table to grab her sister's hands. "And you're doing so good Cissy, even better than before. You look beautiful again." She adjusted herself in her seat. Her eyes and face were no longer red. "Maybe we can help each other out."

"Help each other out?" Caroline asked and leaned back in her chair.

Ginny sat up straight, placing her hands on the table. "Caroline, I am offering you a new start, and I need time to get better and find my way. Just like Dr. Johnston said, if I'm not together, I cannot be there for others. Dr. Johnston said it, and you know it's true."

"What do you need, Ginny?" Caroline asked. "You sound more like someone with a plan than someone in sorrow."

"Well, can't I have both?" Ginny shot back. "Don't be cross at me Cissy."

Ginny leaned forward. "I need nothing. I'm talking about us helping each other," she said pragmatically. "You can watch the kids at Mom's or back at your place while I get myself settled. They love you Caroline and besides," she paused and looked away. "I just don't think I can do it anymore."

Caroline was too lost in her own thoughts to concentrate on what Ginny said. She looked back to the stand of pines and, without thinking, the words came out of her mouth. "Sure Ginny, I'll do it." She knew she was ready as she heard herself say it.

In just over a month, Caroline moved back to Jasper and took over Ginny's waitress job. She moved into the sprawling house that Ginny shared with their mother and rented out the farmland she owned from her marriage to Lee.

Not more than a week after Caroline moved in with her mother and Ginny's kids, Ginny left for the mountains of northern Arizona with a man she had known off and on for a few years. They knew him around Jasper as Plains Jake, a desert cowboy who claimed he could find work anywhere, except in Jasper it seemed. Caroline gave Ginny a tight hug and a kiss on the cheek as they said goodbye.

Years lazily drifted by.

Kin became humbled by Caroline's inner-strength and dedication to Ginny's children. His role of protector and mentor diminished and the time they shared soothed them both. Each intuitively knew how the other felt without having to say much. Silently and steadily, their affection grew

Gospel Sal

1964 - Near South Chicago

Kin could never have imagined how his life would change or how his faith would be tested when Lee Pratt walked into the Mission in 1954.

Even though he knew he shouldn't have had the expectation; Kin felt that God let him down. He believed God would intercede on Lee's behalf. As the years passed, Kin had concluded that he was not close enough to God to have received direction. It was a thought he either confronted with anger or hid from. His doubts caused him to wonder how often he had been wrong, without knowing. As a result, he questioned everything he knew to be truth.

His questions and his doubts systematically and rhythmically returned to him like ocean waves. During the low tides, he could hardly feel them. During the high tides, when the waves started to crash - he could barely breathe.

Kin's wife Theresa was unable to understand her husband's slow descent into himself or his devotion to

42

Caroline. Kin could not see or comprehend how lost he was as the things he knew and loved fell apart and away from him.

Their marriage succumbed to the crashing waves.

There was a time when they both tried. Then, a few years back, there was that day.

"Kin you drink too much and you're too quiet. You care more about other people, more about Caroline." Theresa's voice trembled. Her body shook. "I don't feel like I'm married anymore. You feel far away and refuse to get help." She stopped and took a deep breath to collect herself. "The conversations go unresolved and I'm struggling to find a reason to stay," she concluded as they sat at the kitchen table.

Kin said nothing and silence filled the room like it had weight.

Her words played over and over in his mind; *I am struggling to find a reason to stay; I am struggling to find a reason to stay.* While Kin focused on her words, the ticking from a wall clock became louder and louder. The second hand violently shook and collided with the silence over and over. "All this from a clock that never runs on time," Kin said under his breath.

Theresa looked at him blankly. "There are some things you just can't get past," she whispered. Steel eyed, she stood up from the kitchen table and stared ahead. Looking at nothing and remembering everything, she repeated her words. "There are some things you just can't get past." That was her way of asking for comfort, for him to make it better, for him to want to make it better, or at least tell her it would be all right. She needed him to redirect her thoughts, to at least want to.

"Sit down Theresa," Kin said.

She sat. They stared out the window across the room to an open field. Theresa looked back to Kin. She looked down to her hands, across the room and back out the window. "Well?" she asked, looking to Kin.

"We need a reset, like the clock," Kin responded, still looking out the window. "It shouldn't be this hard," he added and turned to Theresa.

"Our marriage is like a carousel," she said, "we sit apart and go around and around, never coming away with the brass ring." She looked at Kin as he continued to stare out the window. "Jesus Christ, we don't even try."

"Brass rings are for suckers," he replied, still looking out the window.

"What?" she shot back, offended by his comment.

"I have spiritual debt," Kin answered. "It's nothing you can help with."

"Aren't you being a bit dramatic? Is that your plan to stare out the window until things miraculously change?" she asked.

"Dramatic," Kin repeated and chuckled softly. He shook his head. "Sure, dramatic."

The talking stopped. They continued to stare out the window, each knowing their journey together was over, neither able to help the other anymore.

"You should leave," Theresa said seriously, breaking the silence.

"I need to go at it on my own," Kin responded.

"Go at what?" she asked.

"I don't know," he said, stood up, and left the room.

Six months later, Kin sat on a bar stool, with his closest friend in Chicago, convincing himself that all his losses have given him freedom.

Growing up, Kin and Sal Atwater were part of a trio that included Kin's cousin, Betty Anne Chris. They grew up on Kent Island, a place Kin's mother described as, "The place where the land and the marsh become the Chesapeake Bay." To the three, their days growing up on Kent Island felt like different lives, lived by different people.

Betty Anne left during her last year of high school. She moved to England and married an actor she met while sailing on the Chesapeake Bay.

After high school, Kin and Sal headed west. In New Orleans, they rented a small room to keep expenses down. After only a few months, Sal was persuaded to leave, advised to do so after sleeping with the mistress of a local gangster.

Kin woke one morning to find a note left by Sal that read: *It's too hot down here, heading west, catch you down the road. If anybody asks, you don't know me.* The note wasn't signed.

Kin stayed in the French Quarter the next few years. He took various odd jobs, even earning extra money boxing, bum fights at their best. From New Orleans he made his way to Jasper, Texas.

After leaving New Orleans, Sal moved on to Las Vegas and then Seattle before settling in Chicago, always making his living in the bar and music business.

Kin and Sal were different in almost every way. Kin was whiskey; Sal was Tequila. Kin was Gospel; Sal was the Blues. Kin stood like an oak, and Sal swayed like a willow. Kin broke silently, and the pieces were hard to find. There were pieces of Sal all over the place.

Sal has sold his bar, The Gospel, a club he's owned for over thirteen years in Near South, Chicago, a stone's throw from Chess Records. Sal opened The Gospel in 1950, the same year that Billboard changed *Race* records to *Rhythm and Blues*. The Gospel advertised *Booze, Spirits and Blues.*

Addicted to opiates Sal and his wife Evie were ready to start a new life in Mexico. Their new life was financed from the sale of the bar.

It was after hours on the last night of the Gospel. Kin slammed an empty shot glass down on the bar while Sal said goodbye to his last patrons at the front door. "Yeah, it's been a damn good run," Kin heard Sal tell them from across the room.

Kin looked around the empty bar and back to Sal as he walked back. "I can't believe you're letting this place go," he quipped. "What's so damned important about money, anyway?" He sighed. "Just things that gather dust I suppose," he said, accepting the fate of The Gospel. Kin's voice rose. "You know Sal, there comes a point where pain does not affect you personally. You understand that your pain is no worse or greater than anyone else's," he philosophized. He paused and spoke again. "It's the great equalizer."

Back behind the bar, Sal folded his arms across his chest, leaned back and smiled. "I don't know, that's some shit, tell me more holy man?" he asked and then laughed.

Sal leaned over and tapped Kin on the shoulder, nodding towards the end of the bar. Sitting at the end of the bar was a young Buddhist who had quietly and happily worked for Sal the last few years. He cooked, washed dishes and became Sal's in-house confidant. "This guy listens," Sal said in a loud whisper. "He's patient and wise. He's a Buddhist. I can talk to him and get it all out."

Kin looked over at the Buddhist, who noticed Kin's glare and returned it with a large, toothy smile. Kin looked back to Sal. "Maybe he only knows about ten words and has no idea what the hell you're talking about." He tapped his empty shot glass on the bar. "What's his name again?" he asked.

"His name is Five," Sal answered as he filled Kin's shot glass. When I first met him he talked some fifth generation, ancient Chinese shit that kept sounding like five, so, what the hell." He spoke as he walked down the bar to Five.

He stopped across the bar from where Five sat. "This is my Man. I love this guy," Sal said looking back to Kin, "Give me five, Five!" he yelled out and threw his hand out over the bar. Five threw his hand out in kind, slapping Sal's. "He's a brother Kin. Even the black dudes say so." He walked back to Kin, shouting back to Five over his shoulder. "You can pack the flatware and plates. Do what you want with them." Five smiled, hopped off his stool and headed into the kitchen without a word.

"That guy talks too much," Kin sniped, downed his shot and shook his head.

"Yeah, well, there's been a lot of shit going on," Sal confessed while wiping his hands with a rag. "But these Buddhist," his voice broke as he struggled to finish his sentence, "they're fucking amazing." He paused and grabbed the Tequila bottle he'd been filling Kin's shot glass with. "You know, this is my best Tequila I'm wasting on you."

Sal was a clear piece of glass, transparent, razor sharp, and breakable. His conversations were not harmonious. His music did not gracefully progress from one movement to another. Sal's conversations and statements crashed into each other, crashed into those around him.

"Evie was struggling with the pills," Sal confessed. "I was taking them too, just to get through, I guess. It got ugly, more than you would want to know. Heroin too," he admitted.

Kin looked at Sal without saying a word.

"Don't even," Sal said, responding to Kin's stare, "the way you've been putting 'em down. No one would guess you to be a preacher."

Kin looked down at his shot glass and thought for a second. "Maybe I'm finding myself," he said, looking back to Sal. "Maybe possibility *is* my commodity, like you wrote to me."

"So, you are finding yourself." Sal encouraged.

"Fuck no," Kin shot out. "What the hell's wrong with you Sal? I'm sitting right here. I know exactly where I am," finishing his rebuke with a laugh.

"Ok Kin," Sal laughed back.

Sal's mood changed; the cadence of his speech picked up. "What about the Queen, Betty Anne? What's going on in England?"

Kin's eyes narrowed. "You can write her just as easily as I do," he answered.

Sal nodded.

Kin stretched out his arms and yawned. "She's okay," he said, mid-yawn, "still a widow, still living in the country. She thinks I could get a job over there. We write about me visiting."

"Shit, why not!" Sal blurted out.

Kin responded by tapping his empty shot glass on the bar.

Sal filled Kin's shot glass and talked out loud to his thoughts. "A lot of memories," he said looking across the bar, "good and bad." His mind drifted and his voice rose. "They have no issues with any of it," he offered, "I mean they just accepted us. They're helping us."

"What are you talking about Sal?"

"The Buddhists," Sal replied. "God love 'em." He looked at Kin, making sure he had his attention. "I've been going to these meetings every week. If you can believe that shit."

Before Kin could reply, Sal changed the topic. "Hey, remember that book you sent me. What was it called?"

"Dharma Bums," Kin answered and finished his shot of Tequila. He dropped the empty shot glass on the bar. "Kerouac," he added.

"Yeah, right, you know I couldn't get through it then," Sal remembered out loud. "I never thought of you in that way, but I kept it, read it a while back though."

"Yeah?" Kin asked with feigned interest.

"Equally empty, equally to be loved, equally a coming Buddha," Sal recited proudly. "Do you remember that?"

"I do," Kin answered.

"I love his stuff. I read *On the Road* too. Whatever happened to that guy, Kerouac?" Sal asked.

"Well, I suppose he's probably drinking somewhere too," Kin replied with a smile, "maybe a hole in the wall like this place."

"Well then," Sal announced, pouring two more shots of Tequila, "for Jack."

"Indeed," Kin gave back.

They raised their shot glasses and tapped them together. "To Kerouac," they said in unison and downed their shots in a single gulp. Their empty shot glasses hit the bar as one.

"You know," Sal said as he turned and tossed the empty tequila bottle in the trash. "I might want to do something like that."

"Do what?" Kin asked.

"I don't know," Sal responded timidly. "Maybe write some."

"You should," Kin encouraged, sliding his empty shot glass across the bar. "You might just be that type of guy."

"That type of guy?" Sal asked, taking the glasses to the sink.

"That type of guy," Kin repeated, saying it like it was neither good nor bad.

Through the front window, Sal watched an old man curl up on a stoop across the street. The image triggered a concern for Kin's future. "So what are you going to do from here?"

"What's with the questions?" Kin asked. "I'm trying to have a good time here."

"What's the big secret? I was just wondering that's all. You always have something going, faith, God," Sal reminded Kin as his voice trailed off.

Kin shook his head and reached into his pocket for his wallet. "Faith?" he asked. "It's a little unstable." He stood to better reach his wallet. "And unreliable, if you're interested in my opinion."

Sal stood speechless, feeling like he wanted to use.

Kin stared at Sal as he continued. "It's over-rated," he said, daring to be challenged.

Sal stood in awkward silence while Kin pulled out his wallet and started to open it.

"What are you doing?" Sal asked sharply.

"I don't know," Kin responded. "Relax Sal."

"Once a spiritual alchemist, now a spiritual antagonist," Sal offered in a low voice. "New beginnings for both of us, I guess."

"See!" Kin exclaimed, "A writer."

Sal said nothing.

Out of nowhere, Sal remembered the gift he had been waiting to give Kin for months. He regained his excitement and reached under the counter. "I got something for you. I have two. One for me and one for you." He grabbed a small satin bag, and slid it across the bar to Kin.

Kin hesitated. He sat back down on his stool, looked down at the pouch, now in his hand, looked back to Sal and then back to the pouch.

"You can open it," Sal said, half laughing, half demanding.

Kin pulled the pouch open as if it held a hand grenade. Inside was a pendant made of brushed silver with a Buddha on one side and a lotus flower on the other.

Sal, one of the few who knew Kin's real name, caught his eye before he spoke. "Paul, I'm going to Mexico. You're always welcome. Mi casa es su casa."

While Kin examined the pendant, Sal waited for a response like a little brother looking for and needing affirmation.

Kin collected himself, took his eyes off the pendant and looked at Sal. "I don't know what you said there in Spanish, but if it has anything to do with a goat, I'm not in," he said.

Serious looks turned to smiles, smiles turned to laughter.

"Everything is good," Kin re-assured Sal.

"Everything is good," Sal confirmed.

La Fe

It was sunset. "It's that split second," Sal said to the man who stood next to him. The old Mexican smiled. Sal looked down at his hand and positioned his first and second finger about an inch apart. "It's that split second," he repeated with squinted eyes and wrinkled face. He needed to be understood. A lifetime of collected wisdom, as he saw it, in only a few sentences.

The man said nothing, and Sal continued.

"It's a hot August night, the air is thick and you sit in your house and sweat. You step outside and a cool breeze washes over you. It brings the sounds of cicadas and the feel of the ocean. It soothes you." He paused and looked back down to his hands. "And just for a split second," he said with authority, snapping his fingers. "You fall into it. It's just like that." He smiled, satisfied his words expressed his thoughts. "It's being able to let go without losing yourself."

The old Mexican looked at Sal without expression.

"Faith," Sal exclaimed, he insisted.

54

Sal's growing philosophies have comforted him through his darkest moments. They have provided shelter while he aimlessly searched for redemption. Silence, spectacular still waters, weed, peyote and alcohol framed his visions and thoughts.

With notebooks scattered below his hammock, and wisps of light and dark clouds over his head; Sal dreamed, thought, and wrote as blues, oranges, reds and yellows danced between the sea and the sky.

The Light of Waves

I am done with commonplace conversations and tiresome thoughts. Ideally, commonplace conversations would focus on music, high ideas, art, the funniest thing you have ever heard, beautiful places, and good goings on. Conversations would happen in the sun, under the stars, on the plains, in the mountains and anywhere near the water.

I'm tired of and despise sickness, killing, ignorance being late for work, hate, fear and the suffering they bring. Yet, here I remain, here we remain, anchored by responsibility and slaves to the mechanics of living.

My good friend Spin and I happily talked over each other as we drove to the concert. We talked about free will, brain development, neural pathways, and reactionary responses. Everyone called him Spin. He was one of the most together people I knew. In between the brain talk, we fit in pieces of our days and people we knew.

When we arrived at the venue, he looked at the line of people outside, looked down, sighed, shook his head, and laughed to himself. I could hear his thought. *Why in the hell did I let him do it to me again?*

From inside the car, we peered out at brick buildings that leaned into the street. Against the brick buildings, characters of all kinds shuffled across cracked sidewalks and chipped asphalt. Crooked street lamps, perched above like vultures, cut cones of white light that held mist and smoke of all kinds. Hundreds who had suspended their sanity for the night stretched down the street and around the corner. They owned the street. We got out of the car and filed in.

The man in front of me was younger and a foot taller. He wore an Army jacket covered with patches of every kind, had long blond hair and glasses with one shade black. I didn't know why his glasses were like that and didn't ask. When he turned, I just nodded, a silent what's up, I see you. That's how you handle yourself in those situations.

The show was more out of control than the last time. Boots were thrown from the balcony, and beer was sprayed from shaken beer bottles. A thrown beer bottle exploded against a wall near me and started a fight. I saw a man picked up by his neck and thrown into a wall. We left early. Our clothes reeked of beer, and there were shards of glass in my hair. Who says music doesn't move people.

We drove home in silence. Our collective cup was full from our experiences of the night and our previous brain talk.

It's the next day. I'm talking to her again.

"Are you sure you want to leave?" I felt I had to ask, even though I knew the answer.

"Yes, I have to," she replied.

"Let's think on this one for a while," I said, "make a measured decision." I knew it was an impossibility, but still felt compelled to at least try.

"You threw me out of the room." Her voice went cold.

"I thought you left the room. I thought it was a mutual thing. "I meant it when I said it.

There were good times, though. I remembered our trip to the mountain town and the café where a blind man played the piano and sang. He filled the room with magic, mesmerizing dozens of people at a time. It was more than just music. You could smell it, taste it, and feel it. A woman who sat to the front was in rapture. She didn't love the music; she was in love with the music.

There's a difference.

We watched as she waited for him and discovered that the little man was her husband. She was his wife. He was blind, small, and feeble, and she was larger and able. She put his jacket on him with loving care, and he was appreciative, happy, and grateful.

"Now that's love," I remembered telling her as we watched them leave the restaurant. I don't remember her reply, only their inspiration.

That night we drank wine on an outdoor balcony and drunkenly talked of love until an early morning mist crept into the valley. The fog left with the sun, our infatuation for each other not far behind. She needed someone to take care of her, and I needed a muse.

Happiness and despair approach each other on the street. They stop and politely exchange pleasantries. Their act of civility is just that, an act, a feeble attempt to show the other they are above it all. Each scoff at the other's vanity as they walk away. Each shakes their head, feeling no pity for the other.

At the sound of a hollow knock, Happiness forces a smile, says nothing, walks across the room and opens the door to see Despair. They acknowledge each other as they usually do. Despair lets herself in as happiness leaves without looking back. I don't take either of them seriously. They always return.

It became Thanksgiving, and everyone was somewhere else eating, laughing, feeling bloated, doing dishes, and wishing they were somewhere else. I was going to see the Bean.

It had been over a year since the Bean, and I stopped hanging out. I was busy with her, and that was something the Bean did not appreciate or understand.

The Bean was a Bohemian, a guitar player. He stood six foot four, with brown hair past his shoulders and a beard that was graying. When he spoke, he would look over his reading glasses that sat at the edge of his nose. In his early fifties, he was still an imposing figure.

The Bean lived simply and talked freely. He was anti-social, over-bearing, highly intelligent, and utterly comfortable in his own skin. He had it all figured out and would be the first to tell you so.

"Hey man, I'm not feeling like jamming today, but you're welcome to hang out," he said, walking away from me. He stopped, turned, and looked me over. "I guess acoustic would be cool." I went to my car and retrieved my acoustic guitar before he changed his mind.

Bean had an old, meandering dog that would, depending on his mood, bite for no reason. It was funny to the Bean. He understood the dog, and I understood why he understood. I kept a close eye on both of them as I walked by with my guitar in front of me. Both took silent satisfaction in my anxiety.

The Bean and I talked about music and the different ways it hits you. I wanted to tell him all I had learned and thought about as I strummed and practiced minor pentatonic scales. Instead, he plowed forward, educating me. We discussed the books he was reading and his expertise in history.

"See, this is a must read," he informed me, pulling out a historical text. "The way to do it is to read about three books at the same time period, at the same time. I don't read one and then the other, oh no," he said, letting me in on his secret. "What you do is read about a specific event, go to the other books and read about the same event to compare how each was written." He looked over his glasses and wiggled his finger in the air as he told me his secret.

"Yeah, the different perspectives," I confirmed, wanting to show I understood.

"Yeah, that too," he said, running his hand through his beard like a twelfth-century philosopher. His response, only a placeholder while he thought of what he would say next.

That Thanksgiving, we discussed things not commonly discussed on Thanksgivings. The Bean lectured on the Revolutionary War, our State history, and guitar players. I learned how jazz was outlawed in Germany during World War II. He explained how jazz music carried idealistic ideas of democracy and anti-racism in the 1950s, whereas Rock-and-roll focused more on rebellion. That was how it was explained to him from the Jazz horn blower who lectured at the local college. "Pursue music as pure art only," he said, summarizing the horn blower's lecture.

The Bean wasn't a Jazz nut. He appreciated integrity. He showed me all access stage passes he received working with the stage crews, business cards of important people he knew, Presidents of Philosophical

Societies, business owners, politicians, musicians, and radio people.

"I know this guy," he said, pointing to a local professor's business card. "We're working to have a park designated as a national landmark," he paused, "for historical significance man. And this guy," he went on, pointing to another card, "he may have just found treasure researching a sunken ship. He's being financed by some cat from Portugal, big coin man, big coin."

The living room we occupied was large and comfortable. Music had been played in the room many times by many people. Three big easy chairs loosely lined one side with guitar stands near each chair. Across the room were a series of windows, a stool, a few wooden chairs, amplifiers, and microphones on stands. A stone fireplace sat at the far end, and a large table was at the near side, closest to the front door.

The table held mail, articles, and carefully written thoughts and songs. Bean's handwriting was perfect. I suspected, without saying, that he respected the written word as much as the historical figures he talked and read about.

The room looked ramshackle, but not so. A protest sign, signed by a past Vice President of the United States, sat in a corner. Historical artifacts, maps, handouts from Folk Festivals of years earlier, VIP passes, hundreds of CD's and other significant and eclectic memorabilia were scattered on the table and about the room.

Bean put on Super Sessions with Mike Bloomfield, Al Kooper, and Stephen Stills. The song Stop hit me. I got lost in it and placed my guitar on the guitar stand. There was no turkey or stuffing, just smiling and not wishing I were somewhere else. Bean followed up with Roy Buchanan's, Hey Joe. The loud music pressed up against the walls and windows of the house, begging to be let out into the cold November air.

Two girls came over, hippie girls. The girl I knew was named Breeze. She played guitar and sang. Her friend sang along and looked at her like she was a fan. We were all high, and before I left; they asked me to take a picture of the three of them. We went outside, and I took the picture with Bean in the middle, towering over the hippie girls. He looked up, to the side, and up to the heavens as I took the picture. It was as if he was acknowledging a light shining directly on them. And wouldn't you know it, looking at the image; there was, in fact, a stream of light hitting him squarely.

Maybe the Bean had it all figured out, I thought to myself as I said goodbye to the three of them.

On the way home, I received a call from The Monk. With no real effort, I'll spend the winter holiday in the sun. "Good," I replied, "just a few more weeks." Things came together as if they were meant to be. It made me feel connected.

The days and nights mindlessly revolved around each other. I wasn't moving towards December. December came and got me.

It was an early Christmas morning. We had been on the road for over two weeks. We traveled down the coast, meandered west into the Blue Ridge Mountains, back east, and then south, through the Carolinas, Georgia, and south to Florida. I was with the Monk.

The Monk didn't know I thought of him as a Monk. He had never said anything religious or even spiritual. However, the Monk was the only one I knew who had said nothing negative about anything or anyone. As far as it concerned me, he was a Monk.

We traveled without music through Virginia and mountains of West Virginia. Going through the Carolina's we listened to Frank Zappa. Through Georgia, we listened to ZZ Top and Little Feat. In Jacksonville, the Sun greeted us and like loyal disciples, and we put in Skynyrd through central Florida. Led Zeppelin was played the rest of the way. We listened to music like old heads.

It was nice to be received with such hospitality by the Monk's friends. We ate, laughed, and reminded ourselves it was Christmas. The Monk stayed with his friends. My own space was an eleventh-floor room and balcony that overlooked the Atlantic. They dropped me off at the hotel with a backpack stuffed with clothes, a half case of wine, and an acoustic guitar.

The next morning, I woke in the dark, walked down to the beach, and walked into the ocean as hues of orange and maroon infused the nearby clouds. I walked out and stood knee deep in the Atlantic like a farmer from the Midwest, seeing it all for the first time. I watched as our sun, our star, rose over the horizon like it was in a hurry to get to the sky.

Back to my room, I indulged in some inspiration and played guitar on the balcony perch that overlooked the Atlantic. The phone rang. The hotel manager had received a complaint about my guitar playing, "What time is it, anyway?" I asked.

"7:25 in the morning," she replied. "Some guests like to sleep in late. Can you wait until after nine?" she asked.

Sweet anonymous rejection.

Thoreau said it best, "Time is but the stream I go a-fishin' in." That was my intention to cast my line and chart my path over the next few years. What Thoreau forgot to mention was the bait to use. I had all the necessities for my own fishing; my guitar, my writing pad, wine, William Blake, Kerouac, the Sun, and the Ocean.

The Monk was nearby if I needed a ride and my friend, Sean, the minstrel, would appear at a nearby club.

After my sweet rejection and some William Blake, I walked along the beach. Small shorebirds, Plovers, made feasts of tiny morsels the receding waves left behind. The little Plovers stayed ahead of me as they ate. In small groups, moving back and forth with the surf.

The tenacious little birds occupied my mind as I walked from the beach up to Main Street, where I settled in at an iconic biker bar. I met a beautifully tattooed Mom from New Jersey who took no shit as she served drinks. I met a Vietnam Vet and thanked him for his service. We bought each other drinks, and he introduced me to a local luthier who knew all about guitars and name-dropping. We laughed, talked, and drank the afternoon away.

The next day, after my sunrise ritual, I found myself in a blues club where I met a tall, lanky, black man named Moses. He wore an untucked, silk button-up shirt and played an American Telecaster through a Fender Tweed Deluxe. No pedals, just gain. He was a Taoist.

He reminded me that not only was it the New Year, but soon the Chinese New Year. "The Year of the Dragon, the Water Dragon specifically," he explained. He put his drink down and looked at me, studied me. "The Water Dragon is less selfish and less power hungry. He knows when, where, and how to apply pressure." He paused and looked me over to gauge my reaction. "You need to concentrate your energies on the most rewarding endeavors," he finished.

I looked at him in disbelief. "How would you know to say that to me now?" I asked.

Before I could anoint him as a wise man or a sage, he laughed and reminded me, "Remember, this is for everyone this year, you are not so unique after all."

Any feelings of uniqueness I had spilled all over the floor. "How can you do me like that?" I asked. We laughed on and off over the next few drinks.

Our conversations turned to music. "Look, man," he said with a smile, "what do I need to sing for? There's no way I can sing as well as my guitar." I appreciated the simplicity of his philosophy. With nothing to add, I agreed and nodded.

Lifelong friends are born from such conversations, I thought to myself.

A few nights later, I discovered Moses practiced what he preached. His guitar playing was an extension of himself; there was not a wasted note or inflection. I remembered his words as I watched him play. "Everything single thing you do expresses who you are."

Days passed. My fingertips were slabs of soapstone, my guitar, my companion, and wine my comfort. From my perch, I watched in the interplay between the sun, the ocean, the clouds, and the sky. I settled many things in the parts of my mind that are the hardest to reach. This happened subconsciously as I watched multitudes of colors, collected and shared between the ocean and the sky. I watched them through the day and into the night as I strummed an old acoustic guitar.

It was my last night before I was to head back home, and Sean was in town. "No one lets it go like Sean," I yelled to Moses as we watched him perform. People screamed as he strummed his acoustic guitar with abandonment. We watched him sing. We watched him preach. He jumped, and he went down to his knees. We watched as he gave himself over to every moment, every note. We were stunned and happy as everyone around us.

After the show, we stood to the side as Sean talked to locals and those who had driven hundreds of miles to see him. An impaired man staggered up, held out a napkin, and asked sheepishly, "I drove hours to see you. Can you please sign something for me?" Sean looked embarrassed and smiled. "Sure man, what can I sign?"

"Hey!" Moses uncharacteristically yelled out as he reached in his pocket for money. "Sign him that poster on me." Moses looked at me. "My man would give him a kidney. I may as well buy him a damn poster."

The minstrel, the drunkard, and the Taoist.

The show was over, and Sean and I were each headed back north the next day. We walked outside of the club with Moses. It was still dark, and there was nothing to do but sleep.

"Let's drink and catch the sunrise?" I asked and accepted their silence as approval. We meandered toward the sounds of the ocean, passing under street lamps and by neon, storefront signs that buzzed.

It intrigued Moses how Sean could completely let go performing while being shy to speak in conversation.

"Your tipping point, your demon is talking—not performing?" Moses asked Sean.

"I can't explain it," Sean answered. "I've never had an issue with letting go when I play. If I'm a weirdo or a freak when I do—then so be it."

"I get it. You need open spaces, like good music," Moses replied.

Sean shrugged a reply, and the conversation died down. I started to feel salt in the pre-dawn air as we walked toward the beach.

Within a half hour, we were sitting in the sand. Small groups of people, also waiting to welcome the sun, were scattered along the beach. It was still dark, and the moon was soon to give herself over to the light.

"Tell me," Moses asked, looking to the ocean. "What color are the waves, the ones breaking right now?"

Sean and I looked at each other.

"Can you see them?" Moses asked again.

I looked at Moses. His gaze was locked on the incoming waves. His silence demanded a response.

I looked back at the waves. "They're black, dark," I responded.

Still staring out at the dark water, Moses continued. "But you know they're really, blue and green and white and brown. You know this because you have seen them in the light." He paused for a moment. "But some only see the waves like this and think they're always dark."

We remained silent and watched the waves. And no one said a word as the Moon disappeared over the horizon, sunlight took the day, and the waves became blue, green, white, and brown.

Falling inward in Kisatchie

1965 - Kisatchie, Louisiana

On a quiet evening, after a Texas rain, Kin and Caroline said goodbye. For the first time, Kin held her hands, pulled her close, and embraced her.

"I have to go," he whispered, "I am so proud of you."

"What now, is there anything else?" she asked and tilted her head against his chest.

"It's simple," he said, squeezing her tight. "You'll continue on."

In his mind, Kin's path forward was simple. It was math. "There is a process, and there is a result. You work through the process, and you come out the other side with a result. That's what they call experience," he would say.

Kin imagined his goal to be more learned. He was too proud to say he wanted to be happy, too proud to admit he was not. He would often say, "There are no shortcuts."

Sal would often reply, "It's so damn easy to say."

Dear Sal

,

Thanks again for putting me up in Chicago, being able to enjoy the last nights of the Gospel. I'm hoping you and Evie are getting settled and Mexico is treating you well. I want to know more about your place, write more next time. I read your last letter once but lost it. Since I don't know when I'll be able to visit, tell me again about the place and how the people are down there.

Thanks for getting the seminary certificate for me. It helped!

I'm in Alexandria, Louisiana, working as an Assistant Pastor for a Baptist Church. I'm covering for a Pastor who's on a mission trip. The pay's not much, but I get to live in a small house in the Kisatchie national Forest. Remember, New Orleans? Even though this is Louisiana, it's different. I'm in the woods, small swamps and rivers are all around me. Besides the Pastor work and a few half days a week painting houses, I spend time in the Kisatchie Forest. I've met some folks out here that I've taken walks with, but usually, I'm out on my own.

The house where I stay came with a canoe. Canoeing on the Saline Bayou is a religious experience in its own right. Saline Bayou is a sprawling river with dark water. I canoe in the morning, fewer bugs.

It's all got me thinking, though. You moving to Mexico, my life, what's going on with Betty Ann—it just all keeps on moving.

I guess it's a good time for me to be here thinking it all through.

An older parishioner at the church talks about leaves as lives, how they live and die, and how they think they fall into an abyss when they fall away. He explains how the abyss actually feeds the tree. He takes about twenty minutes to go through the entire story (which I have patiently listened to a half-dozen times). It just sounds like dust to dust to me.

But I have to say: I am looking at these damn trees and all their leaves in a forest that's probably been here forever. I have been thinking about the trees and the leaves, growing and falling year after year after year— just like people, falling inward. How is it we never really notice these things? We see them fall; we see them come out; we see them age, but we really never think of it.

If we have all these leaves and lives growing and falling away, what is our abyss? I'm going to do a sermon on that very subject.

Shakespeare says the fault is not in our stars, but in ourselves. He's right. We don't know what the hell is going on for sure.

It's inherent that we don't know Sal, that's all I know. The key is to be able to be held by nothing but a breeze, as a leaf would - to have that much faith.

Hoping one catches you —
Paul

Sal was both happy and worried about his friend.

Quiet Desperations

1967 - Bognor Regis, England

Deep meaning can attach itself to good or evil, inspired, or impaired ideas. Sometimes, feeling needed can become more meaningful than the idea itself.

Soon after Kin's Associate Pastor position in Louisiana ended, his mother passed. Kin traveled back to his childhood home, Kent Island, to preside over his mother's funeral and help settle her estate. It had been years since he had been back. The funeral service was small and unemotional. Settling the estate was simple. Everything went to Kin's brother Michael, save two acres along the bay that went to Kin.

Kin and Michael sat on an old picnic bench that looked out across the Chesapeake, talking of the old days and new days to come. As they spoke, they tended a fire Kin had started from branches he cleared from his two acres.

"I can still remember you and Betty Ann," Michael said.

"Yep," Kin grunted. "She always had her eyes set on bigger things, met her husband right over there, after high school," he said, pointing out to the Bay. "He was from England and couldn't sail for shit. Her and Sal found 'em on the water. He was some years older than she was."

"The actor," Michael interrupted, "he was famous right?"

"To some extent," Kin answered. "A stage actor. I never knew him, only from what she wrote. She said nice things, you never know."

Michael opened two bottles of beer and handed one to Kin. "I never got to know her. Mom always said she thought she was English, that she never came back home to visit."

Kin took a sip from his bottle and looked out to the Chesapeake. "We all make our own way. She came back a few times, years ago." He turned to his younger brother. "You know how it is," he offered, "we make our own lives, sometimes our lives make us."

"I suppose," Michael replied. "Mom also said you were both loners."

Kin reached over and clinked his bottle against Michael's. "Here's to loners," he confirmed.

"So what happened with her?" Michael asked. "No one talks about her."

"You know," Kin let out, replying to his own thought. "This might be the first time we've sat down and had a beer."

"It is," Michael acknowledged, leaning over to re-arrange branches in the fire.

"Anyway, Betty Anne," Kin caught up. "Not much to tell. We were kids, from there mostly letters. How well do you know someone through letters?" he asked philosophically.

"Were there a lot of letters?"

"There were," Kin replied.

Michael fired another question. "Is she coming back now that her husband has died?"

"Hasn't mentioned it. Actually, I may go to England." Kin said nonchalantly. "She said there's an open position at a church near her."

"Really," Michael blurted out in excitement, "back on the road for you, I guess."

"Maybe," Kin said, looking out to the bay.

Michael watched the fire and took a sip of beer. His voice went low. His gaze lifted from the fire and out to the Bay. "I'd do anything to get out of here sometimes."

Weeks later, an agreement was made for Kin to work in Bognor Regis, England as a Lay Minister. The contract was from September to September. If mutually agreed upon, time could be extended. They hired him solely on Betty Anne's persistence with the lead pastor of the Church.

Kin remained in Kent Narrows until he left for England. While he waited, he worked clearing his two inherited acres of underbrush and re-acquainted himself with his brother and his family. At night, he wrote to either Caroline or Sal.

Betty Anne wrote Kin of her love for Bognor Regis, the small hamlet along the English Channel. "It is a beautiful place to grow old," she wrote. In another letter, in a moment of despair, she revealed her darkest secret to Kin. She confided that a Scottish drifter who lived in the countryside had raped her on two occasions over the last year. She wrote of how the only Constable in the area feared the Scottish drifter, which sealed the fate of those in the Hamlet. "People in Bognor are constantly on alert as the Scot spreads his wrath among those who cannot fight back. I think of getting a gun and taking care of him myself if he comes back," she wrote. "There's both a peace and a quiet desperation in the countryside," was how she ended the letter.

Kin replied as he thought he should when he wrote back. "Regarding the other issue you mentioned, I implore you to exercise great caution. Work within the law and pray to God for protection, strength, and grace. Pray for this situation to be removed from your life and above all, trust that the will of God will eventually prevail."

He thought about every word he wrote, "Exercise great caution, pray to God, seek grace and to trust Gods will." He obsessed over what he wrote. All he could think of were the words that were missing, justice, and resolution.

Sometimes sacrifice fuels purpose and sometimes purpose fuels sacrifice. Kin's sense of meaning and renewed purpose was born in Bognor Regis, England.

He determined this could not be left in God's hands alone.

Kin wrote his last letter to Betty Anne and sealed it in an envelope. He instructed Michael to wait three weeks after he left to send it. The closing of the letter read, "You will not hear from me again until I see you face to face in late August."

On a muggy morning in late July, Kin boarded a bus to Haslemere, a small town between London and Bognor Regis. Haslemere was an hour's drive to Bognor Regis.

In Haslemere, Kin rented a room in an old boarding house using the name Anders Kerr. For a few extra pounds a week, a car was made available to him. He stopped shaving and carried a slight beard for the first time in his life. He felt like a different person, a person with a purpose, an objective without examination.

After two weeks of occasional driving and searching, a black motorcycle with an empty sidecar raced towards Kin as he was driving. Kin's heart raced, and his hands gripped the wheel tighter as the Scotsman drew near and passed by in a blur. Kin saw the driver's large red-beard as he flew by. He knew it was the Scottish Drifter from Betty Anne's description.

Once the Scotsman passed by and disappeared over the hill, Kin turned his car around to follow. His heart continued to race as he tried to drive without being seen. In the distance, Kin saw the Scotsman turn off the road to an old gardener's cottage. He noted the area and drove by without being noticed.

A week of anxiety and procrastination, a stormy night, and Irish whiskey came together in a way that felt like nerve, that felt like purpose.

Heavy rain pelted the roof and windshield of the car as Kin drove to the Scot's cottage. No other vehicles were on the road. He pulled over a few hundred feet past where the Scotsman's garden cottage sat off the road, flipped the car lights off, turned the key and shut down the engine, leaving the keys in the ignition. Kin opened the fifth of Irish whiskey he brought with him and took a few sips from the bottle. He put on his collar, opened the door, and put his coat on in the pouring rain. He was completely soaked within a few short moments of leaving his car.

The cottage, which was overgrown with Wisteria, sat under towering Elm and Ash trees. Each raindrop fell hard and heavy against his face as he walked Kin walked the slight path that cut through tall grass and led to the garden cottage. With each step he took toward the cottage, his feet sank into the earth. He could smell the earth and the bark of the trees. Smoke from the cottage woodstove, held down by the rain, lingered in the air. An ominous orange glow escaped from the open spaces of the cottage, around the cracks of the door and from around a piece of wood inserted inside the front window. His heart beat harder and faster, the closer he got to the cottage.

Finally, Kin stood motionless before the heavy door. Rain pelted him. His heart beat out of his chest. He took a deep breath and knocked hard three times.

The door flung open. Kin took a step back in the mud when the Scotsman stepped into the doorway, filling the opening completely. He wore work pants and suspenders over his bare chest. He towered over Kin. "What do yer want?" He growled, looking past Kin to see if anyone was behind him.

"I seem to be lost," Kin answered, trying to speak over the rain. "I need help."

"Enter!" The Scotsman commanded in a hard Scottish accent. His voice cut through the storm.

He turned his back to Kin and walked toward a small wooden table that sat in the middle of the room. On the table was an oil lamp that threw off a dim glow of light. Next to the oil lamp was a large knife stuck into the wood tabletop. The knife blade reflected light from the small fire in the woodstove.

Kin followed. His eyes moved from the Scot's back and scanned the one-room cottage. A handmade bed sat against the right wall. Across from the bed, in the right rear corner, was an open wood stove with a wooden chair next to it. Shelves that covered the wall on the far left surrounded a makeshift sink, with a hose for a faucet. The shelves held food, papers, books, and tools. The floor was made of wood planks, and the ceiling was the underside of a slant roof with exposed beams.

"Sit," the Scotsman bellowed and pointed to the chair next to the wood stove, "it'll dry ya.'"

Kin walked to the table where the Scot sat and placed the opened fifth of Irish whiskey next to the knife. He said nothing and walked to the chair that sat next to the woodstove.

"This?" the Scotsman asked.

"I would never ask for help or enter a man's house without a gift," Kin said as he dried his hands over the woodstove.

"Hmph," the Scot let out, "I don't get company in the wood." He unscrewed the cap and took a swig from the bottle, slapped the bottle down on the table, and jerked his knife out from the wood tabletop. He ran his thumb and first finger across the blade of the knife and smiled through his thick beard. He turned and took an apple from a basket on a shelf behind him. "You scared mate?" The Scotsman asked.

"Should I be scared?" Kin replied.

The Scotsman sliced a thin piece of an apple with the oversized knife and ate the slice from the blade. He smiled as he chewed.

"I built that," he barked out and pointed to the woodstove with his knife. He leaned forward and gestured Kin to take a drink from the bottle.

Kin leaned over, grabbed the bottle, and took a sip. "You do fine work," he complimented, focusing more on the over-sized Scotsman than his own words.

"Some would be scared mate," the Scotsman boasted.

"I imagine most would," Kin replied.

"But you're not?" The Scot asked and stood up abruptly. Kin stiffened as the hairy, shirtless Scotsman turned to retrieve two pieces of Oak for the wood stove.

He walked by Kin and fed the logs to the fire. The knife sat on the table.

"Hey," Kin shot out as the Scotsman walked back to his table. The Scotsman turned, ready. Kin looked up and calmly handed the bottle back without reacting to the Scot's abrupt move. The Scot grunted, grabbed the bottle, and sat down.

"It doesn't matter if I'm scared," Kin informed the Scot.

The Scotsman ignored Kin's comment. He took a swig from the bottle, reached for his knife, and placed the bottle on the table in front of him. "Say again?" The Scot demanded while slicing another paper-thin slice of apple with the oversized knife.

"I'm a man of God," Kin announced, studying the Scot.

The Scotsman loosened up. "Yer off yer heid!" His words were mixed with wild laughter as he leaned towards Kin and handed him the bottle.

Kin took another small sip and handed it back quickly. "I am." He stood and started to take off his overcoat, "Do you mind?" he asked.

"G' on," the Scot grunted.

Kin removed his overcoat that covered his black shirt and collar.

The Scotsman laughed aloud, "A man of God in my house. Pure dead brilliant!" He took another gulp of whiskey. "Aaahhh," he let out, wiped his beard and laughed, "whiskey from a man of God." He sang it.

Kin didn't react. He waited for silence. "A man of God, just as much as you are," he said to the Scot.

The Scot leered as Kin took another swig and laughed even more. "Amen Vicar!" he sang out, tilted the bottle back, drank more whiskey and burped loudly.

The Scotsman no longer shared the bottle. He held it like an infant as he started to talk. "My name is Peter, Vicar. I am a Scot. I don't like the English, and I'm king of this Shire." The Scotsman spoke of his heritage and told wild stories of his lineage and how he was exiled from the Highlands.

Kin said nothing. He noted the changes in the large Scotsman; He noticed his aggression, noticed his sloppiness.

"I don't think I care much for Yanks either," the Scot drunkenly laughed and ran his fingers over the blade of his knife. "You be trying to rob me, aren't you Vicar?" the Scot asked. "You never said where you needed to go," he said, staring at Kin with suspicion. His head swayed back and forth as he sat.

"Bognor, I am headed to Bognor Regis," Kin replied as clearly as he could.

"Bognor!" the Scot screamed out. He rose to his feet, laughed and slammed the knife blade down into the tabletop with force. The knife stuck into the table. He took another big gulp. Whiskey dripped from his mouth, into his beard, and on his chest. "Dry as a bone," the Scot announced and slammed the bottle on the table.

"Well then, which way is it to Bognor, King Peter?" Kin asked, keeping his eye on the Scotsman while putting on his still wet overcoat.

"I'm mad with it Vicar!" Peter shouted and laughed wildly. He leaned in and put his face close to Kin's. His eyes were wide open as he continued to laugh. "Tell me, Vicar," the Scotsman taunted, forcing Kin to take a step back, "will you awaken in Bognor or in the arms of your Lord?"

Kin said nothing.

The Scot drunkenly walked across the small room and opened the door to the pouring rain. "Come, Vicar," the Scot ordered.

Kin walked toward the door while the Scotsman looked out at the hard rain. As he passed by the table, Kin pushed the knife forward and pulled it from the tabletop in one fluid motion. His legs quivered the moment he slipped the blade up into his coat sleeve.

Everything seemed exacting. Kin's focus narrowed. He studied the Scotsman, how he walked, how he moved. He could smell the smoke from the fire, the whiskey, the smell of the room. He felt the moisture through his bones, the tension through his body.

Peter, the Scotsman, walked into the rain as if it were sunshine. He sloshed through the mud in bare feet and no shirt. Mud slopped up against his legs as he stomped in the rain and stopped underneath the outstretched arms of an ancient Elm. Kin, a few steps behind, caught up and stood in front of the Scot. The knife was face up in the sleeve of his coat.

The falling water that cascaded from the Elm's leaves differed from the sounds of the wind and torrents of rain that surrounded them.

"Bognor is north!" the Scotsman yelled out, pointing up the road. "It'll do you good to never show yer' face in these parts again Vicar," he snarled. "The next time it's yer' life."

"You were right, Peter," Kin screamed over the sounds of the pouring rain. "I didn't come for directions."

Peter angrily grunted, "Aahh-"

"I am here on behalf of Betty Anne Chris," Kin continued.

"Who?" the Scotsman demanded.

Kin spun the knife in his hand, gripped the handle and squeezed it hard. "I know what you've been doing, and it stops now," he shouted. His body shook. His heart pounded. The knife was ready.

The Scotsman grunted again. He moved closer, looked down at Kin, and reinforced his delusions. "I'll tell ya'," he screamed. "I am King. I do what I want. I go where I want, and I take what I want." He pounded his first and second fingers into Kin's chest with each word. The hits from his fingers felt like punches from a normal man. Kin moved his right foot back to support himself, to keep from falling backward.

Peter, the bearded Scotsman, the aggressor, continued to move closer. "That's how it be and will be until the day I die. Ye' no whit ah mean?" His eyes were wide open and bloodshot.

Kin looked up to Peter. "Yes, I know," he seethed.

Peter made a move to lunge, and Kin reacted in an instant. He shot his arm back and spun the knife in his hand. He thrust the knife upward in a quick, clean, fluid motion, driving from his right leg, plunging the knife into Peter's belly, right under his chest.

The pupils of Peter's eyes expanded immediately. He gasped, instinctively grabbed Kin's throat with both hands and started to squeeze. His giant hands covered all of Kin's throat and neck. Instantly, Kin could not breathe.

Under a hundred-year-old Elm, with rain pouring on and all around them, Kin and the Scotsman were locked eye to eye. Each man grunted, and their eyes bulged as they fought to remain upright. Kin felt he could die at any second.

Blood trickled out of the Scotsman's mouth. Kin felt the warmth of blood, separate from the rain, on his hand that held the knife in Scotsman's belly. Peter the Scotsman squeezed Kin's neck harder. Close to losing consciousness, Kin twisted the knife. The Scotsman gasped, his eyes rolled up, and he fell forward. Kin moved to the side but not quick enough as Peter, the Scotsman, the tormentor, the king of the Shire, fell face down in the mud, taking Kin down with him.

Kin thrashed in the mud. He coughed and tried to catch his breath as he struggled to free himself from under the Scotsman. He screamed in the rain and the mud from exhaustion and shock, shaking so violently he could only get to his knees. Minutes passed as Kin shook and screamed out while on his knees. He staggered to his feet and stood over Peter in the darkness, in the pouring rain.

He saw the knife to the side of the lifeless body, picked it up and staggered through the mud and tall grass to the car. Near the car, he pushed the knife, blade first, into the earth. He saw a stick and pushed it against the knife handle to drive it down further. Kin stomped his foot over the small hole in the ground and threw the stick into the woods. Still shaking and coughing, he staggered to the car, got in, and turned the key. The engine sputtered. He turned the headlights on and slowly pulled away.

Kin did not leave his room for two days. He lay on his bed, drank water from the bathroom sink, and listened to the rain. When he could finally look in the mirror, he noticed black, purple, and yellow bruises around his neck.

On the third day, he put on his only turtleneck and drove out to get groceries. His body still intermittently shook. He stayed in his room for another four days.

While Kin was getting his groceries, the Constable was dispatched to the garden cottage. Constable Andrew Perry knew the place and the man. He arrived at the cottage to find Peter, the one who had intimidated him, the one who flaunted his defiance, face down in the mud and dead.

Flies buzzed around the lifeless body as the Constable crept closer. He steadied himself. With apprehension, he pushed Peter onto his back with his foot. He jumped back when he saw the Scotsman's wide-open eyes and mud-caked face.

While Constable Perry stood over the body, he scanned the immediate area. He noticed the cottage door was open. He noticed there were no distinguishable footprints near the body. Looking down, his eye caught something half buried in the mud. Constable Perry kneeled down and pulled a priest's collar from the earth.

A neighbor who had seen the Constable's car along the road stopped and walked toward the scene. Constable Perry slipped the collar in his pocket as he stood up to face the approaching neighbor. The neighbor walked up and looked down at the Scotsman's lifeless, muddy body, his open eyes, and the flies buzzing around him.

"Bout' bloody time," the neighbor remarked, turned and walked away.

Six days later, a clean-shaven Kin arrived at Betty Anne's doorstep. She froze as she immediately recognized him through the screen door from her living room.

Neither Kin nor Betty Anne said a word. They stood apart, looking at each other through the screen door. Decades of thoughts, well wishes, Christmas cards, and soul-searching letters had brought them to this moment.

"Well, are you going to just stand there?" Kin asked. "I have a suitcase and everything," he said with a smile.

Betty Anne walked across her living room, opened her screen door, and threw her arms around Kin's neck. "Well, it's about damn time," she said, hugging him tightly. "It's good to see you," she whispered in his ear.

It was in her living room while they had coffee when Betty Anne mentioned Peter's demise. "Kin, do you remember the man I told you about, the man who had-" she paused, still uncomfortable to say it, "broke in those few times?"

"I do," Kin replied.

"Well he died," she said, and quickly took a sip of coffee. "I prayed for him to go away Kin. But I never thought." She hesitated. "Someone murdered him."

Kin reached over and squeezed her hand. "It sounded like he was a bad man from what you wrote. There's no telling what may have happened, or why. Live by the sword die by the sword," he said. "Did they catch who murdered him?" he asked without interest.

"No," she responded quickly. "The Constable told me everything though," she paused, "how they found him in the mud." She took another sip of coffee. "At least he won't hurt anyone else," she said. "I'm relieved."

"Then that is good news," Kin affirmed and tried to change the subject. "Michael and I talked about you and-"

"I don't know Kin," she cut him off, "do you think it was the will of-" she stopped, unwilling to finish the sentence or the thought.

"That is not your concern," Kin assured her and pulled up on the turtleneck that hid the fading bruises left by the Scotsman.

With no pressure to solve the crime, the idea of a murderer going unpunished still pulled at Constable Perry. He knew that no one in Bognor, including himself, would have confronted the Scot. He had a gut feeling.

Three weeks later, Constable Perry walked into Bognor Methodist church for the first time, to hear the sermon from the new American Pastor. The collar he found under the Scotsman was in his pocket.

Kin's voice carried in the old stone Church as he began his first sermon. "And from Psalms 34:17," his voice echoed, "the righteous cry, and the Lord heareth, and delivereth them out of all their troubles."

Kin closed the Bible and looked out to the faces of strangers. He spoke again, unscripted. "What about quiet desperations? What about the prayers that don't get answered?" The congregation sat uncomfortable and silent. Kin took a breath, put his hands on the pulpit, looked up, and asked, "Can you still have faith is what I'm asking. Do you know that your prayers are being heard?"

The words re-played in Constable Andrew Perry's mind for the rest of the service. He shook Kin's hand before leaving and tossed the muddy collar in a trashcan outside of the Church as he left.

England was a refined, lush green pasture. Kin was a rough, dry Wheatfield. England was gray and cold, and Texas was sunny and warm in all Kin's memories. Within two years, he was back in the States, yearning to see Caroline again.

The only other soul to know about the murder of Peter the Scotsman was Sal, who jotted down his own thoughts.

If a bad man repeatedly causes harm to a woman. And that woman prays to God for her assaults to stop and to be protected. And another man kills the bad man committing the attacks. And even though it is murder, were her prayers answered?

Sal's Riffs

Sal's redemption was elusive as Mexican rain. He had nowhere to go but inside, and that is what he did, thinking he could write himself to absolution.

Addicted to pleasure?
Why not?
To feel good now,
In the easiest way?
Why not?

Enough to ease the pain?
Why not?
To feel better?
To hurt less, to heal?
Why not?

To let me be the one?
Why not?
Remove the fear.

Make you clean?
Why not?

There was no one to tell Sal his writing was good or bad. His writing was a riff. It was the blues. It was jazz. It was the sound of the ocean. His words said everything, and his words said nothing.

Envision a woman, in white lace
Balancing herself on a steel rail
Arms spread like Jesus.

Prayers unanswered yet she remains,
Faithful, strong as the steel below her
Arms spread like Jesus.

Sal sent his poems to a newspaper in San Francisco that occasionally printed submissions from their readers. There was such a strong response to Sal's poems: it piqued the interest of the newspaper's editor, who was starting his own publishing company. A poetry book was born when the editor discovered Sal had hundreds of poems and other writings.

Sal's first poetry book, Just in Time-Rhythm no Rhyme, was published in the spring of 1971.

Thought he knew her 'cause she lived down the
street,
Thought he knew, the way to be.
Hurt became anger before he knew hurt.

She filled his mind, yes; you have the right.
Seduced and intoxicated,
She guided him, hand on the small of his back

Butterflies through a meadow and thicket
Through a small knot-hole in a fence
Revealed universes of things he never seen.

Find a truth, define it, name it, hold it,
Be still, let it come to you.
Or instead, listen to only what she says.

Epiphanies, blind spots, wandering signs,
Soapbox sermons that no one buys
Then faith, only hoping to find a spot to shine.

Pray, pray, and pay for some to slip through
Faith shine on, give it all you got.
Bring it, hit us square, square on the blind spots.

Even though many critics gave the book negative reviews and deemed his poetry hard to follow, a small but loyal following developed. Sal's poems resonated with them. His abstract words gave space to their ideas. A critic who liked Sal's poems wrote, "The collection has an undeniable undercurrent that demands an emotional response."

Within a year, twelve thousand copies of *Just in Time-Rhythm no Rhyme* were sold.

Hate and Love, so close,
See them in the corner.
Happiness, she smiles.
Though you can never hold her.

Dogs and stars, you'd never guess
Which one is a killer?
I told you all I knew
But you never would listen.

Beauty and ugliness
They seat you at their table
Feed you the finest fruit.
But only for a favor

Hate and Love embrace
They call you, come closer
It's time to take a chance.
It's time to choose a partner.

For his wife Evie, he wrote:

It's in the way she loves flowers.
It gives a glimpse.
Of how deeply she loves.

To say the words, love you, without thought
Becomes too common,
Too pedestrian

But man, the way she loves flowers.

She feels the rain, feels the sunshine,
Digs into the earth,
And, grows- with those flowers

The beauty, it's in the growing,
Selflessly connected
Loving more fully

It is all in the way she loves Flowers.

His short story, No Amigos, a touching story of a homeless man in Mexico, was published in a San Francisco newspaper and republished around the country. Hundreds of people wrote back, moved by the story.

On a dirty sidewalk, he crouched against a brick wall on a dark blue folded blanket. A stained beige backpack and a worn, black duffel bag sat to his right. The black duffel bag was half-open. Painting supplies, snacks, and loose cigarettes spilled out onto his blanket. To his left, a ten-speed bicycle with another duffel bag strapped to the handlebar leaned against the same wall he crouched against.
He looked to be in his late twenties. His skin was tanned. Unkempt brown hair reached his shoulders, and his beard was trimmed close to his face. He wore a long

black coat over a t-shirt. His fingers had cracks and dried cuts at the joints, where they bent. The cracks and dried cuts looked like they had been there forever.

Spread out before him on the sidewalk were his creations, drawn on various sized pieces of torn cardboard. The drawings were sparse, fluid, and primal. Each image screamed out its own story in ink, colored pencil, and marker.

"Nice art," I remarked, now stopped, bending over, and looking over the scattered pictures.

"Thanks, man," he said, nodded, looked away and exhaled cigarette smoke. He was smoking a cigarette down to his fingertips.

The smallest piece called to me. He drew it in black ink, on a two by three-inch piece of unevenly torn cardboard. The picture depicted a solitary, faceless figure holding an acoustic guitar with lines emanating from its head. Near him were a cactus, a coiled snake, and a skull with horns. An Aztec Sun was drawn behind him and the words No Amigos were etched below him.

"Can you tell me about this one?" I asked, pointing down to No Amigos.

The street stopped, and everything got quiet as he began to speak. "You know, I guess we all have times when we are alone in life. But then again," he paused and took a drag from his cigarette, "they're valuable."

I continued to gaze at the picture.

He exhaled cigarette smoke and finished his thought. "Some people know," he said in a low voice like he was speaking it to himself.

I nodded in agreement while I studied the small picture.

"I can make a nicer one," he announced.

"What's your name?" I asked.

"I'm from New Jersey," he replied, "I can make a nicer one too if you like it. You can sit if you want," he said, pointing to the sidewalk under my feet. I sat without thinking as he began to draw. This time he incorporated marker and colored pencils into the revised No Amigos. He drew on a four by six-inch piece of beige, linen paper that was cut, no torn edges.

I watched his cracked fingers rotate the paper and draw the faceless guitar player. I wondered where he lived.

He concentrated on his drawing as he spoke. "My name is Tom," he announced, answering my earlier question.

I watched as the picture came to life. The words No Amigos were now across the top. The lines that emanated from the figure were sharper and colored.

"Tell me about the lines?" I asked.

"Creativity," Tom answered. He looked up from the picture looked back to No Amigos and spoke again. Thoughts collect in the mind the same way that water collects in a lake. Thoughts leave the mind in words and actions. When water leaves a lake, it carves rivers through stone and falls over cliffs."

I framed no Amigos. The picture sits on a shelf in my home. It inspires me to words and action while Tom sells snapshots of his deepest thoughts, carves through stone, and falls over cliffs in the dry heat of Mexico.

Sal followed with Full of Emotion, a lighter look at his own anxieties.

I arrived home to find that they were all there, all of them, Joy, Anger, Love, Pride, Shame, Nurture, Laughter, Hate, Surprise, and Analysis, just to name a few. The room was full of emotion.

"Do you believe this fucking guy?" Anger asked the moment I entered the room.

"Right!" Pride chimed in immediately.

Surprise stared at everyone in the room with scary open eyes.

I sat down and slouched down on my couch, too much in shock to think, much less speak.

Anger again turned his attention back to me, "You have been tying your shoelaces wrong for almost fifty years, what the fuck." he exclaimed, He pointed to my shoes and started to laugh.

"That's enough," Nurture scolded Anger and scanned those that were assembled in the room. "Does he know why we are here?" she asked.

Turning to me, she asked, "Do you know why we are here?'

I stared back, not saying a word.

Self-server asked about my angle. Emotionally Charged had been on and off crying and the group of them has told Logic to shut up a half dozen times.

My dog left the room.

The argument seemed to be about whether I knew. They thought I was crazy.

None of them knew about the others. Each thought it was just them and me.

How could they not know?

What did they think I did the times I wasn't with them?

"Well, you mentioned no one to me!" Emotionally Charged wailed.

"Tell us, who do you like the most?" Jealousy asked.

Love did not say a word. She quietly and seductively flashed her eyes. She was beautiful. I became weak.

"Yes, who? Who? Who? Who?" They asked in mixed voices.

I kicked them all out. They never left.

As Sal's poetry book sold, and his published short stories gained popularity, he turned his energies and writings to philosophical thoughts. Inspired by Kerouac, Whitman, Blake, Jesus, Lao Tzu, the Buddha, and Goethe, he wrote by the Sea of Cortez.

His next book, *The Tzu, Freelance Philosopher, Ancestor of the Divine*, was dedicated to Kin.

In the book, Sal identified spirituality as "The fabric we are all woven into." He wrote, "Even the most beautiful strand of the finest silk never knew it was woven into the most spectacular rug that lay in the most beautiful palace, near a peaceful countryside, on a

Godly world, and in a loving universe. That magnificent strand of silk, sadly, only knew it was being walked on."

Sal wrote that spirituality had no boundaries and was available to everyone. His interpretations of long-standing beliefs and concentration on spiritual commonalities reverberated with scores of people.

His proclamation that intent was far more important than truth inspired readers to discover their own truths for the sake of truth. Sal wrote, "In the end of ends all you need is to know that you intended to grow, intended to find meaning, intended to find the truth and intended to know your creator - in whatever form spoke true to you." He proclaimed, "The greatest honor is to be able to say with all honesty, I was willing to do his will. Go beyond yourself."

His spirituality was born from an imperfect man, and his confession of that fact opened the door to all those who were imperfect. "Dare to grow despite your imperfections. Break out into the universe," he wrote. Sal further instructed, "Be honest. Be willing to let go. Be willing to find your own truth and know your truth will always be incomplete."

The Tzu, Freelance Philosopher, Ancestor of the Divine, the book that incorporated spiritual insights, observations, and short stories, was published in late 1973.

One critic called the work, "Pedestrian," and another, "Charmingly accessible for the everyday man who is searching." A notable music magazine described the book as "Blue collar hippie-ism, outrageously written with practical undercurrents." And Sal's favorite review, "Seemingly written in a dream-like state."

Kin's favorite short story from the book was Native Flower, a story inspired by Caroline.

Of all the shapes and colors that try to fit into forms, it's the shapeless ones that concern me most," she says, looking at me contently.

I wait to make sure she has completely finished her thought. "What do you mean?" I ask.

"Well," she pauses and rests her hands on the table in front of her. "They understand themselves, where they fit or don't fit, and they know why." She looks down at her hands and gently taps her fingers against the table. "Oh, they might look nice by themselves when the sun shines through them, but they're still just one color, one shape."

She pulls her hands back to her lap and looks out the window, we both do. Outside the window is a long, slow climb of a grassy hill. The hill holds scattered trees, mostly Silver Maple, some Oak, a few Beeches and a River Birch with peeling bark that sits close to the window. The sky is pale blue and the wind slight. We watch the grass sway on the lazy hill. After a few minutes, she smiles and continues.

"But when you put all of those shapes and colors together, it's really something beautiful." She stops and laughs. "And they can never realize it until after they see it, all the shapes and colors together with the sun shining through." Her words trail off with "mmm hmm."

Her attention turns back to the shapeless ones. "But those shapeless ones, they just don't know where to fit, don't know who they are."

"Why do you suppose that is?" I ask.

Our eyes meet as she turns from the window. "That is something I do not know." She says it genuinely, and with a touch of wonder. She tilts her head, honestly thinking about her answer.

"And what did you say these shapes were?" I ask as she tries to lose herself in the swaying grass. "Oh, I don't know," she says, "people, places, things, thoughts, you know. "

"I see. And the forms?" I have to ask.

She looks at me as if this is something I should know. "Well, they would be situations, events, choices," she says. Her answer is as casual as the swaying grass outside.

I lean in close to her and ask, "You're from around here, aren't you?"

"I am," she answers proudly as her head lifts to the sun.

I lean back to feel the same sunlight. "Have you traveled much from this place?"

Her eyes are closed. "No, I have not," she answers while taking in the sunlight.

After some silence, she speaks. "I am not a black man or yellow man, I'm not Caribbean. I am not an old woman. I am not Native American. I'm not Australian, Middle Eastern, Hispanic, or European in any strong way. I've never been truly oppressed, violently attacked, raped, nor have I done any of those things. I have held no one as they have died and I've never given birth. I have not experienced many things. I can only try to understand. And I can only do so by knowing what runs through these experiences. I know where they are born and where they die. "

She pauses and takes a slow breath.

"I know Love and Fear. I know all they create. I've experienced cruelty and hate and jealousy, rejection, ignorance, suffering, and pain. And, and in the face of those things I've experienced tolerance, forgiveness, kindness, understanding, love, and compassion," she says, ending her thoughts with a smile.

"So you're a native flower?" I ask.

"Of the Earth, " she replies with her face toward the sun and her eyes closed.

Sal's riffs were ocean waves, ripples, circles within circles and stories within stories that only existed to grow and become a part of other things.

The Big Clock of Hope

1969 - Turkey Point, Maryland

Russian Sage, Hydrangea and Rhododendron were in bloom.

David James and Hope Connolly parked in a small gravel lot and walked hand in hand to their favorite spot. With their free hands, Hope carried a blanket and David carried a picnic basket that once belonged to Hope's Grandmother.

At their spot, David and Hope spread their blanket under a lone, Red Maple. The Maple was forty feet from the cliff edge that looked over the upper Chesapeake Bay.

A constant bay breeze drove across the water and up the cliff near where they sat. Osprey and an occasional eagle would sometimes hover in the upwind above the cliff's edge. A weathered white brick lighthouse sat behind them, and the rural coastline was visible across the bay.

After relaxing, Hope continued the conversation that had started and stopped in fits. "Are you kidding me,

David James?" she asked. She laughed and rolled her eyes. "Of course there's something to it," she reassured him. He laughed with her and rolled back onto the blanket.

Hope was the only one who called him David; he was Boat to everyone else. David's first word as a child was boat, which became his nickname thanks to his mother. Boat wasn't just in love with Hope; he was in awe. She was his best friend, an occasional lover, and his muse.

Barely five feet tall, Hope was twenty-four and lightly freckled with piercing, brown eyes. She was strong, temperamental, sometimes poised, and idealistic.

Boat was twenty-two, and not as confrontational as Hope. Still fitting into his own skin, he knew he had much to learn and smiled easily. He painted, but never considered himself an artist.

Hope sat cross-legged in an off-white cotton blouse and faded jean shorts. The sun was behind her, and Boat watched sunlight peek through her long hair as he looked up at her.

She moved closer to Boat, shook his shoulder, and reminded him again, "Don't worry about the word astrology, because," she paused, "it's only a word." She took a deep breath. "Are you ready to listen?" she asked with an exaggerated sigh.

"Yes ma'am," he answered, laughed and leaned back, supporting himself on his elbows. He was a mess of hair and sunglasses.

"Now David, pay attention," she began. "You know you have a personality, right?" she asked.

She looked over and saw Boat had already drifted off. She shook her head and watched as he stared out at the scattered whitecaps that glistened in the sunlight. He hadn't noticed she stopped talking. She waved her hand in front of him. "I knew I shouldn't have let you smoke before we started," she said, tapping him on his shoulder. "Can you be in the right space for this, David James?" she asked.

He turned, said nothing, and smiled.

She leaned over, gave him a soft kiss, and sat back. "So David, like I said, we all have a personality, correct?"

"Correct," Boat replied and nodded, working hard to pay full attention.

"And we know we all have a soul, right?" she continued.

"We do," Boat responded.

As she spoke, they instinctively laid on their sides, facing each other. The wind blew through her hair, and she traced her finger on the blanket between them. "And then there is God, right?" she asked.

"There is," Boat replied, watching her finger.

"And God and the Soul are somehow related but separate, right?" she asked.

"Ok," he acknowledged, giving his full attention.

"So here is your soul," she said, drawing a circle with her finger on the blanket between them. "And personality," she said, drawing a larger circle around the circle she had just traced.

"Ok," he responded.

She drew another circle around the two. "And then this would be God, or whatever, or the entire blanket, you know what I mean?" she asked, looking at Boat for confirmation.

"I'm with you," he said, holding her gaze.

"So if personality is a mind thing, different from the soul," she said, tracing her fingers over the two imaginary circles, "the desires of the soul are separate from the personality."

Boat rolled over on his back, looked at the sky, and thought for a moment. He felt high. Hope still hadn't said a word. He rolled on his side and looked at her. "Yeah, I agree with that," he said, smiling.

Hope pushed his shoulder in her excitement. "So what if the planets, where they are when we are born, affect our personality, just our personality, not the soul," she proposed. "It's a big clock!" she shouted out. "Maybe God set it up that way. Maybe it's some kind of energy, I don't know," she exclaimed. "The planets don't affect our soul, just our personalities."

Hope paused and looked at Boat. "I think our personality is a tool, a way for our soul to communicate. Is that cool or what?" she asked and playfully pushed Boat.

Boat flopped from his side to his back in an exaggerated motion from her push. "Far out," he said, thinking about it more and gazing up at the few clouds above him.

Hope leaned over him. "It's the coolest thing," she said and laid next to him. They stared into the sky. "It's a big clock," she said, looking up. "It's amazing."

"Hope?" Boat called out while deep in thought.

"Yes, David," she responded.

"Do you think you can tell the future by astrology?" he asked.

"Now you're just being stupid," she replied.

Boat laughed aloud as Hope tried to keep a straight face. She gave in, and they both laughed hard, neither knowing why. Boat grabbed Hope and tickled her. They rolled over on the blanket, knocked over the picnic basket and ended up on their backs, breathing heavily and still laughing. Laughter gave way to silence as they drifted back into the clouds.

"David."

"Yes?"

"Are you, my friend?"

"Yes, Hope."

"My best friend?"

"Yes."

"Do you promise?"

"Yes."

"Always?"

"I promise."

He pulled her tight and started to kiss her.

She stopped and turned away. Her back was against his chest. "You can have me tonight," she whispered. "I just want to lie here with you now."

Angels watched as the young couple held each other, trying to figure out the universe, trying to figure out themselves.

Dr. Gerard will See You

1970 - Bethesda, Maryland

She stood up from her desk and walked to the sliding glass window that separated the receptionist area from the waiting room. "Dr. Gerard will see you shortly, Mr. Sage," she said with a slight smile. "If you don't mind," she said, politely motioning for Kin to take a seat.

"Of course," Kin replied. He turned, scanned the empty waiting room. He looked up at the dirty, drop ceiling and down at the grey carpet. *Typical, uncomfortable, waiting room chair*, he thought to himself as he sat down.

The chairs in the waiting room were made from chrome tubes and maroon fabric. They lined the waiting room walls, wherever there was not a door. The walls were light blue. Each wall in the windowless waiting room held a wood door. All the doors were dark wood except for the entrance door. The entrance door was a full-length filtered glass. Perspective Counseling, Suite 202, was etched in the glass.

As Kin sat, he listened to the receptionist answer the phone. "Perspective Counseling, how may I help you?' she asked dozens of times.

Minutes later, the door next to the reception area opened. "Mr. Sage?" a thin man asked and walked to Kin, "Nice to meet you. I'm Dr. Gerard," he said, introducing himself.

"Pleasure," Kin replied, shaking his hand.

"Please, follow me," Dr. Gerard requested. Kin followed him down a hallway and into his office.

Dr. Gerard's office looked exactly how Kin imagined a psychiatrist's office would. There were diplomas on the wall, a couch to the side and shelves full of books. The overhead fluorescent lights were turned off, and lamps were used to light the room.

Dr. Gerard walked to the side of his desk. "I hope you weren't expecting something too formal," he said as he walked behind his desk. He motioned Kin to have a seat in one of the cushioned, high-back chairs facing the desk.

"Do you mind if I loosen my tie?" Kin asked, "I'm not really a suit guy."

"Take it off," Dr. Gerard responded flatly and quickly. "Actually, I expected you'd be wearing a collar."

"I rarely wear a collar unless I'm working." Kin replied as he took his seat. "It puts people off."

Dr. Gerard opened a folder and leafed through Kin's application, resume, introduction letter, and references. "Kin, now that's an interesting nickname, how did you get that?"

Before Kin could reply, the Dr. continued. "Let me tell you more about what we're looking for. Our team goal is to assist service members coming back from Vietnam. For the most part, we facilitate education and work opportunities as well as assist those who struggle." Dr. Gerard paused, leaned forward in his chair, placed his forearms on his desk, and continued speaking. "The staff Chaplain would interact with a variety of faiths and philosophies. How do you feel about that?"

"I have no issues," Kin replied. He reminded himself to be cautious, not too opinionated. *Only comment on the specific question asked* Kin thought to himself.

"So you are not tied to any religion?" Dr. Gerard followed up.

"I don't feel the need to convert someone to a particular faith or define a person's perspective. So no, I am not tied to a particular religion," He leaned forward and rested his forearms on his thighs. "There are enough commonalities in all of them."

Without any reaction to Kin's response, Dr. Gerard leaned back and thought for a moment. He reached forward, grabbed his reading glasses, and picked up one of the scattered papers on his desk. "I see that you were in England. How was that?" he inquired.

"Different," Kin replied.

"And, Texas before that?" Dr. Gerard asked. He flipped his reading glasses on top of his head and leaned back in his chair. His body language told Kin he expected more information.

"Well yes," Kin started, "I was located in Jasper, Texas for several years. I ran a non-denominational church and for the most part, ministered to the community at large. I did most things you'd expect, Sunday services, baptisms, weddings, funerals, some counseling, support groups." He paused, making sure he had covered everything, "and community groups," he added.

Dr. Gerard flipped his glasses back down from the top of his head and continued to review Kin's documentation. "You provided counseling services?" he asked, "I don't see that listed."

"Not official counseling," Kin replied. "I should have said that I counseled parishioners."

"Are you married?" Dr. Gerard asked as he tossed Kin's paperwork onto his desk.

"I am not," Kin answered automatically.

"Are you willing to share why?" Dr. Gerard followed up, switching into psychiatrist mode.

"Hmm," Kin let out, "I'd say there were a thousand reasons. It was something that," he paused. "Well, unfortunately, it just happened."

Kin's mid-sentence pause triggered Dr. Gerard, "Do you have regrets?"

"Doesn't every man," Kin replied.

Dr. Gerard sighed. "I apologize if my questions are too personal Kin, it's just-"

"I understand completely," Kin interjected, "you need to find the right fit."

"Correct," Dr. Gerard added, "I need to find the right kind of person, because, quite frankly, there's no training. I can't tell you from week to week who you would talk to, what their issues might be, what situation they may be in, what challenges they may face or what they will need to assist. I can only assure you that no one speaks to the Chaplain unless they want to." He made eye contact with Kin to ensure he had his attention. "Consultation with the Chaplain is purely voluntary."

Kin nodded in agreement.

"Good," Dr. Gerard said, confirming Kin's nod as acceptance. "This position provides support only. It does not prescribe care."

Kin said nothing and nodded again.

"So, back to England, how did you find it?" the Dr. asked.

"Wet," Kin replied. He was satisfied to leave it at that but knew the Dr. wanted more. "The people were pleasant, different," he continued. "I was in the countryside working as an Associate Pastor at a United Methodist Church, one of the first in England." He paused and thought of his time in England. "To be honest, it became boring. The people were nice but settled in their ways. My job was ritualistic, everything was routine." Kin looked for a reaction from Dr. Gerard as he spoke. "Maybe I was stuck in a routine," he finished.

"And Texas?" Dr. Gerard asked, digging deeper.

"Well," Kin perked up, "we are talking Texas." He smiled at the thought of Texas. "I learned a lot in Texas, a lot about people."

"Please go on," Dr. Gerard urged.

Words came to Kin without thought. "In Texas, I learned that people only sometimes mean what they say, initially anyway. Most times, it's a response to something. You need to ask questions, give a person time to understand what they want, or even need. I guess it all starts there."

Dr. Gerard tossed his glasses on the desk and folded his arms across his chest. "And how do you feel about the war?" he asked.

"I have no opinion," Kin said immediately. "Debating the issue serves no one. Hopefully, things end soon."

Dr. Gerard didn't respond. He looked past Kin. After a few moments, he asked, "May I share a personal experience with you?"

"Of course," Kin replied, leaning forward in his chair.

Dr. Gerard took a deep breath, looked over to the draped window and back to Kin. "I haven't been doing this for a long time. I was running a private practice in Annapolis, mostly families, and kids." He leaned forward. "My older brother died in the war, and my father was a veteran. So, I wanted to help." He moved, His chair squeaked as he continued. "I was naïve about what I was getting into." Dr. Gerard swiveled his chair toward the draped window. "I love the way the afternoon sun fills those drapes, they almost glow. Don't you think?" he asked.

"They are glowing," Kin confirmed and said nothing else, letting the Dr. continue.

Dr. Gerard took a deep breath. "The man who trained me said that one of the most important things you can do for a patient is to help them establish goals." He looked away from the drapes, to Kin, back to the drapes and continued speaking. "I prepared, all night and the next morning. I went over how I would handle myself, what I would say. It was the first day, and in my excitement, my appointments got out of order. I had the wrong file for my first appointment." Dr. Gerard paused. "I didn't know," he said to himself as his voice trailed off. "Anyway," he spoke up, "when I opened the door to invite, who I thought would be my first appointment, a young man in a wheelchair was waiting for me." He paused again and looked to the drapes. "I guess it stunned me. I'm sure I looked like I was. So, best I could, I regained my composure and bulldozed right into my training. I asked him if he had any goals."

Kin didn't say a word while the doctor spoke. He didn't utter a sound when the doctor paused.

"He said his goal was to eventually walk across the room." Dr. Gerard cleared his throat and wiped a tear from the corner of his eye, trying not to be noticed. He rolled his chair back and cleared his throat again. "Well, anyway," he let out, grabbed a folder, and walked around to the front of his desk, "you just never know, is what I'm trying to say."

Kin stood up as Dr. Gerard walked around the desk. They stood face to face when Dr. Gerard made the offer. "There will be a weekly report you will provide, it would include a briefing on each client. The format is simple. You are not obligated to share anything you feel is confidential unless a client communicates that they intend to hurt themselves or someone else. This position provides two weeks of vacation and five sick days." His tone was flat like he was reading Kin his rights. "I expect you to be available Monday through Friday between the hours of 8:00 AM and 6:00 PM. We meet as a team on Monday mornings at 8:00 AM. Each Friday, you will receive your patient schedule for the following week, some may require home visits. In the event of an emergency, I am confident you will rise to the occasion. Do you have any questions?" he asked.

Kin took a moment to process everything the doctor said. "I have no questions. I'm good," he replied.

As Dr. Gerard leafed through the packet of papers in his hand, Kin asked, "What happened to the kid in the wheelchair?"

"He never came back. I wish I knew," he said as he handed Kin his hiring packet.

Just like Kerouac

As best I can, I will recall the event, the one that started all the confusion in my mind.

I did not realize he was there until he spoke. His words were quick and sharp and directed to me. "The only reason you're not confused is because you don't think about it, and the only reason you don't think about it is because it's too confusing."

"What?" I asked. My mind was not ready for his observations.

"Let's try again," he said. He repeated his words slower and deliberately like I was a child. "The only reason you're not confused is because you don't think about it - and - the only reason you don't think about it is because it's too confusing." He walked over to where I sat and leaned over to get a closer look at my face.

Looking at me, he asked, "Who are you?"

"I'm me," I replied, looking back to him and holding my arms out, turning my palms up.

His response was immediate. "You are nothing," he hissed. He paused, put his hand against his chest and slowly asked, "Who then, or exactly what is me?"

"I don't know me," I replied. I turned toward him and extended my arms out further to show, to express, well, me.

"So, you're a body?" he asked, dragging out the words, over-emphasizing his question.

"No. Not just a body," I responded, feeling like I was being set up.

He sat down across from me. "What else then?" He pretended to be interested, pretended to be patient. He crossed one leg over the other, clasped his hands around his knee, and leaned forward.

"I have a soul," I said, thinking of that first.

"A soul?" he questioned. "Where is it?"

"I'm not sure," I stammered. "I guess it's something you can't see."

He leaned forward. "Why not?" he asked softly. "Why is that?"

"You don't believe in things you can't see?" I asked, answering his question with my own.

He started to speak and then stopped. His eyes narrowed, and he leaned in closer. Dryly and coldly, he asked, "See how, with my eyes, smart guy?"

He was controlled and unpredictable at the same time.

"Yes with your eyes," I replied, just as dry and just as cold.

He didn't respond. His body relaxed. He leaned back and took a deep breath. "Are you upset with me?" he asked.

Not waiting for an answer, he stood up, closed his eyes, and smiled. After a moment, he re-opened his eyes and started to walk around the room, which was glaringly white. "Sometimes I am not so good at all this," he said, caressing his cheek with his hand. He started to pace back and forth. He stopped and turned around.

"Do you dream at night?" he asked as he walked toward me. "Your Mother, who has left her body, do you still see her?"

"Well yes, but-" I froze, trying to figure how he knew my mother had passed.

He took a step back and crossed his arms across his chest. "How so, Mr. Eyes Man?" You could hear the contempt in his voice.

My thoughts went to my mother, how she was when I was younger, years before she passed. "I guess in my brain, my mind?" I said, picturing her as a young child from old pictures I had seen.

"Which one?" he demanded, still standing with his arms crossed.

"What?" I replied, distracted, still thinking of her. I could see and hear her all at once.

"Do you see her in your brain or your mind?" he asked, slowly to make a point. "Where did you see those things?"

"You know what, I don't have time for this shit," I shot back. "I've had enough."

He ignored my response and continued to taunt me. "Why is it too confusing?" he asked.

I didn't respond. I was stuck in thought. I just sat there. He sat too. I have no idea how long, years maybe.

"Are you under the impression you have all the answers?" I finally asked.

He took a deep breath. "Oh, no," he said as he exhaled. "I'm completely at sixes and sevens."

I tilted my head and squinted, puzzled, unfamiliar with the term.

"Confused, at odds," he said, shrugging his shoulders and turning his hands upwards.

I took an open shot. "I'm amazed you would admit to such things."

"I have nothing to offer but my own confusion. Kerouac said that. Do you know Kerouac?" he asked, ignoring my comment.

"I do," I replied.

He leaned forward. "And still I am so much more aware than you," he whispered smugly.

"And why is that?" I countered, unimpressed with his self-centeredness.

He looked at me and waited until we made eye contact before he spoke. "I'm aware of how unaware I am, whereas you think you have it all figured out," he said with satisfaction. He leaned back, closed his eyes, and clasped his hands behind his neck.

"Do you know what vainglorious means?" I asked, tired of his tone.

He ignored my question. "You think you have it all figured out, don't you?" he taunted with closed eyes.

"No, not at all," I answered, my frustration growing.

122

His eyes opened. He smiled. It was the moment he had been waiting for. "Why not, do you just not want to think about it, or is it too confusing?" he asked, holding a tight grin.

I glared at him through him.

"I know, I know, I know!" he repeated excitedly. He stood up and started to pace back and forth over the white floor, by the white furniture, and under white light. He was dressed in all white. And, as I recall, I had trouble distinguishing the beginning and end of things. Everything was so white.

He suddenly seemed anxious. "I'm not so good at this," he said, not nearly as composed as he had been. "You were supposed to ask me. You were supposed to ask the question of yourself. Who am I?" He sat across from me and took yet another deep breath to collect himself. "Trust me, it goes so much smoother that way, when you ask in your own mind."

"And then you appear?" I asked.

"Yes, exactly." his voice rose when he answered like I had been with him all along.

I played along. "Fine, then tell me."

He paused, purposely making me wait. He lowered his voice and asked innocently, "Tell you what?"

"The answer, the truth!" I screamed, ready for the conclusion of this.

He smiled. "But I told you," he said, "I'm at sixes and sevens."

"Really. Seriously?" I asked in a fit and threw myself back against my seat.

It was silent for a long time. Everything was still.

Breaking the silence, he asked softly and sincerely, "Would you be ok at sixes and sevens?"

"What do you mean?" I responded sharply.

His voice was firm and clear. His words were deliberate. "Would you be ok at sixes and sevens?"

"Yes," I said it and meant it.

And he was gone. That was all I remember. It's still hard to distinguish where things started, where they ended, how long it took, or even where I was. It was all very white.

In a flash, I realized that, literally and poetically, we are truly made of stardust. We breathe, we eat, we live, and we die. The trillions of cells that make up our bodies carry the past of our ancestors.

Our existence is physical, mental, emotional, and transcendental. Our mind is separate from our brain and different from our soul.

Our planet revolves around a star that is a part of the Milky Way Galaxy. The Milky Way Galaxy contains over 200 billion stars, is trillions of miles across and is part of a Universe that holds billions of galaxies.

I don't understand how life began. I'm unable to differentiate my mind from my soul or even my own thoughts from what my creator may inspire.

I feel as insignificant as a grain of sand on a hundred-mile beach and as big as a universe, all at the same time.

I am truly at sixes and sevens.

Years went by before she visited me as I slept. "Oh, I see he's at it again," she said. Her smile was kind and patient. I could tell right away she was a spiritual woman.

"I think so," I replied, not knowing what else to say.

She stood against a stone wall. A lush meadow was behind her. I asked about God and immediately recognized how thoughtless my question was.

She didn't answer; there was no need. Her response was only what it needed to be, a sympathetic smile.

"The sixes and sevens are only words," she said, "nothing that should perplex to you. It's thirteen if you wish." She paused. "You must remember, this is the process of growth. Introducing new ideas always introduces conflict." She gave me a moment to absorb what she said before she continued. "The only way to escape conflict and uncertainty is to not grow, which is an available option. But you seek to understand. Is that not true?"

"It is," was all I could muster.

She understood my difficulty and continued. "Answers to questions will be known as you grow and move toward more enlightened ideas." She gave a sympathetic smile. "You thought it would be easier, didn't you?" she asked.

"Yes," I answered, finally able to respond.

"We all do," she offered.

"What can I do?" I asked.

She gave me a long look before she spoke. "Live loyally, let enlightened ideas, become enlightened actions. Be flexible and be steadfast." She spoke with compassion and clarity. "The truth never changes; it waits for you."

I realized that, just like Kerouac, I also had nothing to offer but my own confusion. With nothing of real value to offer, I asked, "Who was that person talking to me, who put me in such a way with the sixes and sevens?"

She looked lovingly at me as she spoke. "That was you, my dear." Her words sounded like music, and I watched as she slowly disappeared from my sight.

Socrates of the Sand

It was sunrise. Sal looked out to the sea of Cortez. He looked down to the notebook in his lap, and wrote, "Is falling off a cliff or standing alone in a driving rain only the falling, the wind, the cold, the being soaked to the bone?" He looked back and forth between the sea and his written words. He sighed, looked down, and scribbled over what he just wrote. He wrote again. "Is falling off a cliff or being in a driving rain only the falling, being soaked to the bone?" He circled the passage, sighed again, and scribbled over the words. He thought about Kin.

Kin had written to Sal about soldiers coming home, the guidance he gave, and the guidance he imagined to give. Kin wrote that Irish whiskey and Merlot were the most effective in regulating how much he took in at a time. "I don't know if I'm making a real difference," Kin wrote, "in the long run, anyway." In another letter, Kin wrote, "They encourage clients to move forward on their own. The disappearance of people I get to know is consistent and unceremonious."

Through Kin's letters, Sal witnessed a man who had been moved to the core. The returning vets, who Kin referred to as kids, changed him. He seemed more solemn to Sal.

"Is that even possible," Sal asked himself when he thought of it, "being changed through the experiences of others?"

Sal put his notebook down and picked up another notebook that held a half-written letter to Kin. He looked out at the sea for minutes, pulled out the letter and wrote, "Is falling off a cliff, or being alone in a driving rain only the falling, being soaked to the bone?" Sal looked up and back out at the sea. He focused on the sky behind the horizon and then down to the letter. He listened to the waves. He felt the sun warming his skin. He wrote again, "Would you feel it if you were falling if you were soaked to the bone? Would you feel it if the waves were pulling you under?" he asked. Come to Mexico," Sal offered.

In July 1973, Kin's position as Chaplain for Perspective Counseling was de-funded. Dr. Gerard had expected the loss of funding and found another position for Kin - if he was interested. One of Dr. Gerard's closest friends, Jeff "Sarge" Sargent was a Prison Administrator in Talbot County, Maryland. Sarge agreed to hire Kin as a Prison Chaplain on Dr. Gerard's recommendation alone.

Even though any job was worth looking into at his age, Kin felt the urge to travel. He needed to see Caroline and visit Sal.

Sarge agreed to hold the job, hoping to finally find someone who would keep it more than a few months.

After a last visit with coworkers and local friends, Kin packed his wagon and headed to Texas to see Caroline. Texas would be his first stop on his way to visit Sal. He felt anxious and alive, entering Texas. His bad memories were infused with child-like excitement in seeing Caroline again.

The reunion of Caroline and Kin was soft, quiet, and intuitive. Caroline listened to Kin's stories, and Kin, for the first time in a long time, felt like he was home. They took long walks throughout the week.

"You know, Caroline, I was thinking, "Kin said as they walked down a tree-covered trail.

"You know Kin, I've been thinking too," she said, softly cutting him off in mid-sentence, "I think in another five years, these children may all be on their own." She knew precisely what Kin was going to say and exactly how to respond.

"Kin?" she asked.

"Yes?" he replied, looking to her as they walked.

"Have you ever thought about using your given name, Paul?"

"Maybe," he admitted with a shy smile.

Kin held on to her hand and stopped walking, turning her towards him. They looked at each other for minutes without saying a word. Kin reached out and caressed her cheek. They kissed for the first time. It was perfect. It was enough.

There was no talk of the future before he left to see Sal, both understanding the future unfolded on its own.

In San Felipe, Kin found an energized Sal. His books had garnered a small but dedicated following. Sal's most profound thoughts, born along the Sea of Cortez, had been edited, printed, and distributed. His thoughts and philosophies had become a product that people held in their hands.

Sal's minor successes enabled him to expand his Paraiso to a small community. He bought additional land along the coast and built huts that could be rented out for days, weeks, or months at a time. Those who couldn't afford rent contributed. They gave jeep tours on the beach, set out umbrellas, tended the gardens, cooked food, and other tasks that helped the small, transient community grow.

Sal was transformed into a more confident, free spirit who gave phone interviews and wrote articles espousing his philosophies. Spirituality provided the joy, money the swagger.

As a by-product of Sal's success and visibility, a small but steady stream of hippies, surfers, searchers, and other wanderers traveled to find Sal, searching for a new way of life. To them, Sal the Tzu, the Freelance Philosopher, knew the next step. Although surprised, Sal secretly reveled in the idea of people listening to him, traveling to see him, making efforts to find him. Sal was being found almost every day.

"Mi casa es su casa!" Sal yelled out, greeting Kin, repeating the very words he spoke the last night at the Gospel. Sal shook Kin's hand and noticed the pendant he gave him that night in the bar. It was attached to a leather bracelet around Kin's wrist.

Standing in the sand, Kin slapped Sal on the side of the shoulder. "It's all looking good Sal, exactly what I need right now."

"Yeah." Sal beamed. "I'm getting a boat too."

"A boat?" Kin questioned.

"A boat and a captain," Sal said proudly, "deep sea fishing."

"No shit," Kin gave back.

"No shit," Sal confirmed. "There's your hut," he said and pointed to the hut near them. "It's the nicest one on the beach. Take a few days to cool out from the drive and relax." Sal turned to leave. "Food is over there," he yelled over his shoulder, pointing to a small thatch-roofed beach-side stand. "Showers and bathrooms are a few huts past it."

"Got it," Kin yelled back as he walked towards the hut. He looked down to the planks placed in the sand. He heard a gentle wave, looked to the sea, and then up to the hut, all the way to the hut. The planks, the sea, the hut. The planks, the sea, the hut.

The hut sat a few feet above the sand. Two steps brought you inside. They wrapped the hut in a screen to keep the bugs out. It held two chairs, two tables, a small bookshelf, and a hammock. The taller table sat between the chairs, and the smaller table sat beside the hammock that was used as a bed. Kin used the small bookshelf for light storage. There was no electricity or running water. Those luxuries were nearby at the bathhouse and the small grill that Sal pointed out.

Kin stayed close to his hut. He looked out at the sea, walked the beach, ate, drank, read, and thought.

On the second morning, Sal stopped by.

"Good morning," Sal greeted Kin, holding a cup of coffee in each hand.

"Morning," Kin replied, "thanks." He nodded, taking the cup of coffee.

"Hey, listen," Sal blurted out. "I need you for something, easy stuff for you, little brother."

Kin looked down, shook his head, and smiled to himself. "Little brother?" he muttered and laughed.

"Yeah," Sal replied. "I got things now, but later today?"

"You know where I am," Kin replied, raising his voice over the sound of the surf.

That afternoon, two young men, both with beards and long hair, dropped by Kin's hut to say hello. "So you two are hippies?" Kin asked with a smile.

"The Tzu told us you were all right," the taller one said as they all sat in wood chairs outside the hut.

"Right, The Tzu," Kin confirmed, amused by Sal's new identity.

"Yeah, the Tzu," the other replied. "Have you read his book?" he asked.

"Yeah well, I have," Kin stammered. His curiosity took over. "You liked it?"

The taller one spoke up again, "Oh yeah, it makes you look at things man, think about things -"

"Well," his friend interjected, "if you're the type who thinks about things."

"I know what you mean," Kin replied.

The three men got quiet, turning their attention to the sea.

"Do either of you play chess? " Kin asked, breaking the silence.

"I do," both answered at the same time.

Sal stopped by as Kin was enjoying conversation and a game of chess.

"Hey, Tzu, Good afternoon, Tzu," the hippies said together as Sal walked up behind Kin.

"Gentlemen," Sal replied, greeting the small group. "Afternoon little brother, ready to take a ride?" he asked Kin.

"Afternoon," Kin replied, "I'm ready." Before he could move, Sal was in front of him, grabbed his hand, and pulled him up and out of his chair.

"See you, fellas," Kin said to his newfound friends.

Walking to a jeep parked on the beach, Kin looked to Sal. "You know, you didn't need to pull me out of the chair."

"Not in front of the hippies?" Sal asked and gave Kin a nudge against his shoulder as they walked.

"Exactly," Kin confirmed and started to chuckle.

On the way to the jeep, Kin stopped before getting in. He raised his voice over the surf. "Sal-"

"What's up, Little Brother?" Sal asked immediately.

"That!" Kin shot out. "Stop fucking calling me Little Brother."

"Such words preacher man." Sal gave back, taunting Kin.

"Yeah, such words," Kin rallied, "and another thing, the Tzu, really?"

"Now, Kin, you've got to understand," Sal said, starting to crack a smile.

"On that note," Kin interrupted. "I'm thinking you can call me Paul from now on."

"What the hell, you change your name but I can't change mine?" Sal asked, trying to keep a straight face.

"Paul is my name." Kin shouted out, laughing as he said it. Sal laughed and threw his hands in the air.

"Ok, ok," Sal continued, "so let me make sure I got this right. So, little brother?"

"No," Kin replied, looking down at the sand, shaking his head back and forth.

"Kin?"

"No," Kin repeated, trying to keep a straight face, still shaking his head.

"How about sweet tits?" Sal asked.

Kin looked up. His face was stern.

"Yeah, sweet tits works," Kin said dryly. His straight face turned into a smile and then, to laughter. "It's good to see you," Kin said, looking over to Sal.

"It's good to have you here sweet tits," Sal responded and jumped into the driver's side of the jeep. Kin got into the passenger side. Sal turned the key, and they drove over the hard sand that was closer to the water. The sea breeze blew against them as they drove.

After five minutes of driving along the sea, Sal pulled the jeep up onto the softer sand, turned back around toward the sea, and turned the engine off. "Listen," Sal said, turning to Kin. "You're partially to blame for this."

"Blame, blame for what?" Kin asked. "You seem happy to me."

"I don't know what to tell these people," Sal admitted.

"What the hell are you talking about?" Kin asked.

Sal sighed and looked out to the sea as he talked. "Look, I didn't know I would write a book much less two, and now people are showing up, looking for some sort of answers." He turned back to Kin. "And I don't have shit. I mean, I wrote what I thought at the time." He spoke faster. "I don't know what else to say. Christ sakes, I don't even know if I feel the same way now."

"Ok," Kin replied.

"What do you mean, ok? Are you listening to what I am saying?" Sal asked with urgency. "I've got people traveling to hear what I got to say and I've got nothing to tell them."

Kin thought for a moment. "Sal, you're a promoter," he thought aloud. "You can't tell me you didn't see this coming." He turned and asked, "Did you invite them down here?"

"Absolutely not," Sal immediately replied, slapping his hands on the steering wheel. "I mean, I don't know," he mumbled as if he was talking to himself, "maybe when I wrote that people should seek their own truth."

"There it is," Kin declared. "That's what did it." He sat back in his seat and put his foot on the dash. "Damn, those poor, confused bastards," he teased.

Sal barely heard Kin's taunt. "Look," he said, holding his gaze out at the sea. "I was thinking. Maybe you can talk to them, say something to them."

Kin jumped out of the jeep and stood next to it. "No, no spiritual advice," he said, shaking his head.

Sal stepped out of the jeep. "What are you talking about? That's what you do," he said, walking to the front of the jeep near Kin.

"Things change," Kin snapped. "Right, Tzu?" he asked sarcastically.

Sal threw his hands in the air. "Well shit, I figured if anyone knew what to say, it would be you. I mean, you're the one who said I should write." He took a second to think carefully before asking. "Is this about that shit in England?" he asked. "We've been over that-"

"Don't even," Kin cut Sal off. "You do not understand what you're talking about. Besides," he quipped, "why am I the one to answer to people who are coming to see you."

"Well, Kin," Sal said deliberately and slowly, "because I don't know what to say. Do you not remember me telling you that?"

Sal walked a few feet towards the sea and sat in the sand. Kin sat where he was, a few feet behind Sal. They both stared out at the sea of Cortez for the better part of an hour.

Kin stood up, walked to the water, and then back to Sal. A smile grew on his face as he looked down at Sal.

"What?" Sal asked, curious about Kin's smile.

"I cannot teach anybody anything. I can only make them think," Kin said over a crashing wave.

"What," Sal asked, "what do you mean?"

"Socrates," Kin exclaimed, trying to prompt Sal.

Sal looked up and squinted against the sun. "Ok, I have no idea what the fuck you're talking about."

"It's ok to not know the complete truth, who does?" Kin asked.

"I sure as hell don't," Sal answered, slowly falling in-line with Kin's thinking.

Kin completed his thought. "There you go Sal, that's how Socrates taught. He asked his students' questions. Ask them why they are here. Ask them what they want," he instructed. "Do you think you have all the answers, Sal, honestly?"

"Shit, no!" Sal screamed out proudly.

"It's the simplicity of it all," Kin summarized, putting it all together. "Tell them that their search does not end with you."

"That's it!" Sal rejoiced, completely satisfied with his newfound position.

"Answers that are not answers," he said to himself, "brilliant."

The freelance philosopher now has something to say, nothing.

"Just be sure to give them a good show," Kin said as he climbed into the jeep, "give them their money's worth." He froze as he heard himself say the words, thinking of the Tent Preacher

There Goes a Preacher Man

1974 - Caroline County, Maryland

Kin watched as Sal applied the Socratic Method to the questions that came his way.

"This is perfect," Sal confirmed daily. "It fits. It really is the next step. How in the hell I didn't think of this, I'll never know."

"Even teaches old dogs new tricks," Kin mused as they drank morning coffee. "Imagine that."

"It shouldn't stop," Sal said. His words trailed off as his gaze drifted out to the sea. "You know, it's just—"

"On that note," Kin interjected, "it's about time I get on the road."

"Already?" Sal turned to Kin. "You can't stay longer?" he asked.

Kin was slow to respond. He took a sip of coffee, savored the taste, and brought the cup down to his lap. "Yeah, I'm going to shoot up and see Caroline, and then see about that job." He looked at Sal, back out at the sea, and took another sip of coffee.

Sal looked out at the sea with Kin, assessing the situation in his mind. "Well, if the road calls," he let out with a sigh.

"It's not that. This place is something else." Kin responded, scanning the immediate area. "It's a paradise," he said, looking at the grill hut, the bathhouse, and the gardens. "But it's not my paradise," he explained, and looked back to the sea, past the scattered palm trees.

"Remember my brother," Sal said before Kin left, "mi casa es su casa."

"You know it," Kin replied, bringing his arm up, making a fist, showing the pendant Sal gave him on his wrist. "Until then," he said and got into his car to leave.

Back in Texas, Kin and Caroline kissed again. She called him Paul whenever they spoke. They did not talk about the future.

In Maryland, Kin arrived expecting to meet Sarge. Instead, Sarge sent his assistant warden, Mark Herald. His meeting wasn't the interview he expected. It was an orientation.

"Most are a little intimidated at first," Mark shouted over his shoulder while Kin followed him through the main block of the second prison. Kin noticed the prisoners looking at him, sizing him up. "It's really not that bad," Mark yelled back and turned around to make eye contact with Kin.

"Not a problem," Kin shouted back.

After the tour of the second prison, they walked to the lot where their cars were parked next to each other.

The assistant warden opened his car and grabbed a manila envelope from the back seat. "You think you can do this?" he asked seriously. As Kin opened his mouth to speak, Mark continued, "It's just a weekly service, some counseling time, and a class at each place, per week. You make your own schedule."

"Can I meet the prisoners when they first come in?" Kin asked.

"I'm sure that can be arranged," Mark answered. "All the pay and benefits information is in here," he said, handing Kin the manila envelope in his hand. "Fill it all out and bring it with you Monday."

"Sounds good," Kin replied and gave Assistant Warden Mark Herald a firm handshake. Kin accepted the job with the thought it was God's will.

"OK, we'll get you going Monday," Mark said as he climbed into his car. He gave Kin a wave and pulled away.

There were no chapels in the two prisons he served. They held services in conference rooms. Kin was now a preacher without a church.

It was his first sermon. Kin sat at the front of the conference room and watched the prisoners shuffle into the room. A few feet in front of him a worn, wood pulpit stood front and center. Kin's Bible sat on top.

Once the inmates were seated, Kin stood. For the first time in over five years, Kin walked to the pulpit. He scanned the room without saying a word, looking into the faces of all those who came.

"Does anyone know what theology means?" Kin asked, breaking the silence. He waited, knowing the first to speak loses.

A voice from the back replied, "Religion and God shit, man." A few laughed.

Kin looked down at the pulpit and re-positioned his Bible. He studied the faces before him and walked toward the section of the room where the voice came from. "It's how religious concepts apply to your lives now," he said, adding to the anonymous comment.

No one responded. Kin turned and slowly walked back to the pulpit.

"Let us pray," Kin instructed and looked out at his newest parishioners. He waited for everyone to close their eyes. Once their eyes were closed, he started. "Father, bless those who seek to know you. Whoever has ears, let them hear, Amen." The prisoners were slow to open their eyes, expecting a much longer and more drawn out prayer. "It's that simple," Kin said. "Ultimately, what you do is your decision, your intent."

For no good reason, Kin's mind went blank. He looked down at the pulpit, to his bible. He noticed the various bookmarks and dog-eared pages. The words, my own redemption, flashed through his mind like they were not his own. He collected himself, looked back out at his congregation, down at his, and opened to the first tab. "Romans 3:23," he said clearly, "for all have sinned and fall short of the glory of God." He stopped and looked back at the group. "We are all truly sinners," he

said sympathetically, "all of us. You just got caught."
Some nodded in agreement, some laughed.

Kin looked down and turned pages again. "John,
Chapter eight, seventh verse," he announced, "Let him
who is without sin among you be the first to throw a
stone." He looked out again, searching for reactions.
"Mathew six, fourteen through fifteen," he went on. "If
you forgive others their trespasses, your heavenly
Father will also forgive you, but if you do not forgive
others their trespasses, neither will your Father forgive
your trespasses." Without looking up, he flipped
through pages to another passage. "Colossians chapter
one, verses thirteen and fourteen." His voice echoed in
the small conference room. "He rescued us from the
domain of darkness and transferred us to the kingdom
of his beloved Son, in whom we have redemption. "

Any feelings of nervousness Kin felt were gone. He
flipped pages to the book of Isaiah.

"Isaiah chapter forty-four, verse twenty-two," he said
with confidence. "I have blotted out your transgressions
like a cloud and your sins like a mist, return to me, for I
have redeemed you." Kin stopped, closed his, and
walked out from behind his pulpit, closer to the seated
men. He stopped and looked at a man in the second
row. "The bible says you are redeemed. Is that
possible?" he asked the man.

"Yes, Sir," the man replied.

Kin walked back to the pulpit and leafed through the
pages to his last bookmarked page. "And finally, Luke,"
he preached. "When these things take place, straighten

up and lift up your heads, because your redemption is drawing near." He stopped, closed the Bible, and looked at the assembled inmates. In each prison, it was the same, silence. He ended his first sermon the same way at each prison. "What's done is done. We're all sinners. You were forgiven before you even asked. So, act as one who has already been redeemed."

He waited a few moments to let his words sink in before he ended the service. "Repeat after me, please. Blessed be the name of our Father in Heaven." The seated inmates repeated his words in low murmurs.

"Amen."

"Amen," they repeated.

Without a word, Kin walked down the middle aisle and left the room. The inmates remained silent, not sure the service was over. It had only lasted fifteen minutes.

Slowly they got up to leave. "Now, there goes a Preacher Man," one said to another as they exited the conference room.

Siren Screaming

1974 - South Chesapeake City, Maryland

It was after midnight. Old metal streetlamps dimly cut the darkness below enough to show the mist hovering above the wet asphalt. Brick townhomes that had balconies over their front porches lined the street. Two blocks downhill, the street stopped at the river.

It was quiet except for the sounds of a police car's lights. Click, click, click, every few seconds, in clock-like time. Blue and red light rotated, painting the sides of buildings and cars again and again. The colors were captured and reflected in the wet asphalt and random puddles. Those who were awake peeked out of their windows.

Two police cars were parked outside of the brick townhome where Boat rented a second-floor apartment. The first had no lights on. The second patrol car was the one with the flashing lights and the click, click, click. Two officers stood and leaned back against the trunk of the second car as they quietly talked.

They heard footsteps, stopped talking, and turned toward the footsteps. Raymond Child appeared out of the mist. "Good Morning Officers, what's going on?" he asked with his hands raised as he walked.

"Keep it moving," the taller, older officer commanded, waving him away.

"Hey, I came to see my man Boat. Is he all right? Something going on?" Raymond asked. He moved towards the silhouetted officers, "I'm cool," he said, keeping his hands in the air as he walked toward them.

The other officer, Officer Pat, was younger and knew Raymond. "Have you talked to Boat today?" he asked.

Raymond relaxed, dropped his hands, and continued walking towards the two. "Butter, man, call me Butter, and no I –"

"Stop right there!" the older officer yelled. He stepped back with his right leg and dropped his hand to his baton.

"It's okay. I know this kid," Officer Pat said.

"I don't give a shit. Come here, kid," the older officer ordered while Officer Pat rolled his eyes.

Raymond followed the direction of the older officer and slowly walked toward him. The older officer grabbed Raymond and threw him against the trunk of the patrol car. Revolving blue and red lights flashed over Raymond as he was roughly patted down.

"Hey man, what about my constitutional rights?" Raymond muttered while being patted down. "Oh, Ok man, I see, 'cause I'm black right, Ok, Ok, you got the badge, I get it?"

"He's clean," the older officer proclaimed, turning Raymond around.

"That's what I get for following directions?" Raymond asked as he re-adjusted his jacket.

Officer Pat walked to Raymond, reached out and tugged on Raymond's jacket, helping him to re-adjust it. "You ok?" he asked.

"Yeah, man," Raymond replied and looked over to the older officer. He looked back to Officer Pat. "What's going on?" he asked in a whisper.

"Have you talked to Boat today?" Officer Pat asked with a sense of urgency.

"No," Raymond answered. "What's going on?" he asked again.

Officer Pat looked up to Boat's apartment as he spoke. "The landlord's wife called. He's been missing since dinner and the last place she knew he was going, was here."

"Shit, Jessie? Come on," Raymond blurted out. "Everyone knows that old man is just out drunk somewhere, shit."

"Maybe," Officer Pat acknowledged, "but we've been here a half hour, and Boat won't let us in or answer his phone." He paused. "I don't want to force my way in, but he does," he said, gesturing his head to the older officer.

Raymond said nothing and nodded.

"I'm running out of options," Officer Pat admitted.

"Well first off," Raymond replied, "you don't get in from the front. The entrance is in the back. Let me go up there?" He looked at Officer Pat and then to the older officer who had just stepped closer. "You know Boat's not like that."

"I say let him do it," Officer Pat said to the older officer.

The older officer looked up at the apartment, back to Raymond and folded his arms in front of him. "What the hell, the quicker we can get out of here, the better," he agreed. "I'm turning these lights off," he said over his shoulder, walking to his patrol car.

"You know me and Boat are cool. I want to make sure he's ok," Raymond said loudly, so the older officer could hear as he walked away.

"Now, you know I can't be responsible if something goes wrong. Let's do this right," Officer Pat warned Raymond.

"It's cool," Raymond replied and turned towards the apartment.

Officer Pat grabbed Raymond's jacket and pulled him back. "Remember, let's do this right."

"It's cool," Raymond replied, straightening his jacket, "like I said."

Officer Pat followed Raymond a few steps and walked to the older officer. Both watched as Raymond vanished in the alley between the two townhouses to the rear entrance to Boat's apartment.

The entrance to Boat's apartment was atop the metal fire escape at the back of the building. As Raymond made his way between the townhouses, the older officer looked over at Officer Pat. "Boat and this one wants us to call him Butter? Does anybody use a real fucking name anymore?"

Raymond quietly climbed the steel steps up to the landing and looked in through the windowpanes of the back door. He saw Boat squatting against the wide archway between the kitchen and living room with his head is in his hands.

The door shook as Raymond knocked. "Boat, hey man, it's me," he whispered loudly. "Boat, Boat, it's me, let me in before those cops head up here, man." He spoke louder to get Boat's attention. "I know you can hear me."

Boat slowly stood up and walked to the door with his head hung down. He opened the door a few inches and placed his foot against the bottom. "You don't want to be here," he said, still looking at the ground.

"Look, I'm here," Raymond said and stuck his arm in the opening. "Let me in, man. What's going on?"

Boat looked at Raymond blankly. He took a deep breath, walked back, and slid back down against the wall where he was. Raymond followed and stood across from him, near the kitchen.

Raymond pulled a joint out of the inside pocket of his army jacket. "I almost got popped for this," he said, holding the joint up. "They gave me a pat down. I think that old man down there likes me," he said and laughed. He leaned back against the wall, across from Boat and gave a kick against the bottom of his boot. "What's going on?" he asked.

As Boat raised his head to answer, Raymond struck a match to light his joint. In the flash of light, when the red phosphorous converts to white phosphorus, when the match catches and creates a flame, Raymond saw two feet and legs from behind the living room wall.

"Shit!" Raymond shrieked. He jumped up and back at the same time. He dropped the match and walked past Boat, towards the living room. He looked around the corner to see Jessie Tyler, on his back, dead.

"Raymond, Boat!" the younger officer screamed from down below.

Raymond ran by Jessie's body and opened the door to the balcony over the front porch. "Hey, it, it's ok, it's cool, just a little mis..misunderstanding," he yelled out, "ju...just, just give me a minute," he stuttered.

"Get him down here, or we're coming up," Officer Pat yelled up.

"I will, sir!" Raymond shouted back and re-entered the living room.

He stood over Jessie, all hundred and thirty miserable pounds of him. Raymond's body shook. Still, he managed to strike another match and light his joint. His hands shook as he walked over to Boat, leaned against the wall and slid down across from him. He took a drag. "Jesus Christ man, I thought you were a pacifist," he said as he exhaled.

Boat looked up, petrified. "I just pushed him off of me, I swear," His voice trembled. His eyes were wide open. His face was frozen in fear and shock.

Raymond handed him the joint. "Boat," he encouraged, "it's ok, it's manageable." He held out the joint, motioning for Boat to take it.

Boat stared through Raymond. "What's wrong with you?" he asked without moving a muscle.

Unaffected, Raymond again motioned for Boat to take a hit. "We just need to relax, I mean it's -"

"You have to believe me," Boat interrupted, his voice shaking, "I didn't mean to do anything. I just pushed him off of-"

"We're coming up," the older officer shouted through a megaphone, cutting off Boat's words.

Raymond jumped up. "Look, that that man is serious," he said to Boat as he ran to the balcony door. "It's cool, just a little situation," Raymond yelled down.

At that moment, Boat took off for the back door.

"Boat!" Raymond screamed at his friend. "No wait, Boat!" he shouted, imploring him to stop.

Boat crashed into the door. His left hand broke through the glass windowpane in the collision. He pulled his hand back through the window, opened the door, and ran down the back steps with blood dripping from his hand. The entire steel structure alongside the building shook as he leaped down the stairs. Vibrations from the metal stairway echoed loudly between the townhouses and into the street. Dogs barked as Boat crashed through garbage cans in the backyard, jumped over a fence, and escaped into the early morning.

"Shit!" Officer Pat yelled as he ran between the buildings after Boat.

"Son of a bitch," the older officer let out as he jumped into his patrol car and took off, siren screaming.

Raymond hadn't moved from the doorway that led to the balcony. He took a step and stood over Jessie's body, the first dead body he had ever seen. His hands shook as he re-lit his joint. "Damn," he said as he looked down at Jessie. "You still look like a mean old man." He walked to the bathroom, took another hit, flushed the unfinished joint down the toilet, walked back through the kitchen, down the steel stairway, between the two townhouses and sat on the front steps. He knew more police would arrive soon. "Keep calm baby," he reminded himself as his body started to shake, "keep calm."

After a few minutes, a patrol car pulled up and parked along the curb, in front of the townhome where Raymond sat.

Two officers jumped out. One went directly to the few people that were talking amongst themselves in the street.

The other officer walked over to Raymond.

"He's upstairs?" the officer asked.

"The dead guy?"

"No, Boat," the officer answered impatiently. "Where is he?"

Raymond sat with his elbows on his knees and his head in his hands. "My guess is Hope's," he answered.

"And Jessie?" the officer prodded.

"Yeah, he's still dead," Raymond said from behind his hands, "upstairs."

"We're going upstairs. Go home, we'll be by in a bit for your statement, understand?" the officer asked.

"Yes sir," Raymond responded, feeling the full weight of the situation

The Paying

1975 - Talbot County, Maryland

It was sunrise. Someone died; someone had to pay. Boat sat with Hope on her front porch when the patrol car pulled up. He stood. They read him his rights, handcuffed him, and placed him into the back of the patrol car as Hope, and her parents watched in silence. They stood motionless as the patrol car took Boat away.

David "Boat" James, twenty-eight years old, was processed at the Talbot County jail and allowed one phone call. Boat's father hung up as Boat explained what had happened. After the call, he was fingerprinted and handcuffed to a chair. The Judge was on his way.

"Please be seated," the Judge announced as he walked into the courtroom.

"I'm guilty," Boat shouted out as everyone took their seats.

"Son, do you understand what you are pleading to?" the Judge asked.

"Whatever I'm being charged with," Boat replied, looking directly at the Judge. His body trembled. His eyes were red and swollen.

The judge sighed and looked around. "I am re-scheduling this hearing for two days from now. And, I want all the information associated with this case on my desk by the end of the day tomorrow," he directed.

Boat entered his cell, went to his bunk, rolled under a cover, and faced the wall. He heard the steel door shut from under his blanket and barely moved for the next two days. When he started to cry, he put a pillow against his face so they would not hear him.

Two days later, he was brought back to the judge. "Sir," the judge stated, "you are being charged with involuntary manslaughter. Do you wish to enter a plea?"

"Guilty your honor," Boat murmured.

"OK then," the judge confirmed, opening a manila folder. "Given you have no criminal background, and this was, by all accounts, unintentional," the judge read from his notes, "you are being sentenced to twenty-two months of incarceration for involuntary manslaughter."

Those were the last words Boat remembered hearing. They took him to a holding room and shackled to a chair while waiting for the van that would transport him to prison. Boat sat alone for hours before the door opened. They escorted him to the rear of the building where the van was waiting. The side doors opened, and Boat was seated with six other convicts.

The van stopped at a tall chain-link fence outside the prison. The gate opened, and the van drove to the side of a building. Boat was taken out of the van with the others and processed into the prison system.

He was the fourth in a line of seven that were walking, single file, to their assigned cells. Each prisoner held his prison jumpsuit in front of him and only wore boxers. It was what they made all new prisoners do.

It was cold. The ceilings were high, and the cinderblock walls were painted white and gray. Florescent lights buzzed from above, and noise filled every empty space. Loud laughing, yelling, talking, banging of steel doors, and now, the taunting of the new prisoners filled the air.

Boat was in shock. He could barely speak. He half closed his eyes as he walked in line, not wanting to see what was around him. His eyes were fixed on the shoulders of the man in front of him, trying to pretend away where he was.

Suddenly, the line stopped without warning. Boat stumbled into the man in front of him. His jumpsuit fell out of his hand. As he bent down to pick up his jumpsuit, multiple voices started to scream and inmates who were in front of him, scattered behind.

"He's a dead man if you don't get back. Now hold it, boy, put it down, put it down, move, get back, man, get back." Words collided, landing on top of each other.

Standing back up in his boxers, Boat was front and center to the confusion and commotion in front of him.

An inmate from the front of the line, Shane Dubrow, from Louisiana, stood behind a Chaplain with an arm around his neck. Shane had smuggled in a small razor and had grabbed the Chaplain from behind as the line passed him.

Boat remembered Shane bragging in the van. "They'll never fuckin' hold me," he told anyone who would listen on the way to the prison. Hours later, Boat was witness to Shane's plan. Shane Dubrow's left arm was around the Chaplain's neck with a razor to his throat. His right hand flailed in the air as he screamed. "Get back, I'll cut his throat right here, right now!" Dubrow's threats echoed through the corridor to cheers from the inmates.

Boat, overwhelmed, stood petrified as one of the prison guards moved closer to Dubrow and the Chaplain. "Calm down, take it easy," the guard repeated, slowly moving closer to the two.

Boat noticed the only one who seemed calm was the Chaplain. He stood with a razor against his neck like he was waiting in a grocery checkout line.

"What now?" the Chaplain whispered back to Dubrow and as the guard crept closer.

"Man, shut your mouth before I cut you," Dubrow shouted in the Chaplain's ear, pushing the flat side of the razor against his neck.

The Chaplain ignored Dubrow's command and replied calmly. "You should tell 'em what you want. That's what usually happens."

Dubrow, confused, screamed to the guard. "Hey, Hey, I want a car. Get me a car, or I will cut old white man here."

The guard paused, and slowly moved closer to Dubrow and the Chaplain. "Just relax, we can work this out," he repeated over and over.

The Chaplain moved back against Dubrow, gently forcing him to take a step back. He whispered back to Dubrow. "Don't let him get too close. He'll try to grab you."

"Shut up, old man," Dubrow screamed in the Chaplain's ear, walking back another step. "Get back Pig," he shouted to the guard.

As Dubrow waved, his free hand and screamed, the Chaplain pushed back again. Dubrow was a foot away from the cinder-block wall behind him. Without Dubrow noticing, the Chaplain pulled his right knee up.

In an instant, the Chaplain explosively scraped his heel down Dubrow's right shin. At the same time, he thrust his left arm against Dubrow's. Dubrow's arm flailed into the air, and the razor flew free. In the same motion, the Chaplain reached back with his right arm, grabbed a fistful of Dubrow's hair, threw his feet out from under himself, and fell like a rock to the ground. Dubrow's head, screaming from the pain to his shin, was yanked down by his hair. His head violently crashed into the Chaplain's shoulder when he hit the ground.

Shane Dubrow, the Cajun who vowed they could not subdue him, flew up from the impact. His eyes rolled back, his head hit the cinderblock wall behind him, and he crumbled to the floor. Blood dripped from his right leg, as he lay on the tile, almost unconscious.

Guards ran over and rolled Dubrow on his stomach. They pulled his arms behind him. One kicked him in his side, and another retrieved the small razor from the floor.

The Chaplain groaned as he sat. He put his palms down on either side of him and pulled his leg back to push himself up.

A guard walked over and held out his hand. "You are one crazy son of a bitch. We could have had him," he said, pulling the Chaplain to his feet. "You ok?" he asked.

"I'll know better tomorrow," the Chaplain replied and patted the guard on both shoulders. Both laughed nervously.

The Chaplain turned and noticed Boat, who never moved from his spot. "You alright?" the Chaplain asked.

"Yeah," Boat drawled, trying to regain himself, now the first in line.

The Chaplain extended his hand. "I'll meet you soon enough," he said with a grimace. "I'm Kin."

The line started to slowly assemble. "Move it," a guard screamed from the back of the line.

Boat replied. "Boat, Sir." He didn't notice Kin's outstretched hand as he started to walk forward. As he walked, he turned around to see Kin talking to the guard.

"Boat, what kind of name is Boat?" he heard Kin ask the guard as the line crept forward.

Continue On

He was an old man by the time I knew him. He called me Kid and sold fruit out of the back of a pickup truck. He peddled produce all over the country, steering clear of the law that would ask to see his permit to sell. He drove a black Ford pickup that could carry seventy-five bags of potatoes that weighed fifty pounds each. He attached black painted plywood sides to the bed of the truck. Dried drips of white paint ran down each letter of POTATOES that were painted on top of the black plywood.

"You could take out a quarter, pull it right out of your pocket, hold it arm's length up to the sun and block out that entire sun with just a tiny, old quarter." Maybe he would have smiled. "I suppose you could block it out with even smaller things too if you held them close enough to your eye."

That's what I imagined he might have said to me if I had a problem. Maybe I would have learned patience and perspective back then. He never did. I never did.

He wore overalls and a wool cap most of the year. He traveled with a dirty, old poodle named Snowball and kept dog biscuits in his pockets, so the dog would stay close. Sometimes we would drive down to the docks to buy the produce wholesale. We would leave early in the morning before the sun came up. On the way, he would stop to buy a coffee with milk and a white powdered doughnut.

As a kid, I knew all the roadside fruit and junk peddlers who sold produce and used anythings they could make a buck on. They planted themselves along the two-lane highway that led to the beach. Coffee, Lacey, Pops, Joe and the oldest, an eighty-year-old man that went by the name The Cheese, were my childhood mentors. The Cheese sold roadside produce in a shirt and tie. As a young boy, I sold fruit with all the old men. I was fair-skinned, freckled, and felt as old as they were.

After dark, the highway became symphonic. Eighteen-wheelers screamed through the night. Each truck became a unique instrument. The sounds of the engines, the tires, the speed, the echoes, and the spaces in between - all unique.

Years went by. He got older, and his big Ford became a Datsun. He made smaller potato signs and did precisely what you would expect. He continued on.

Years ago, my friend Doug created a painting called Dogs and Stars. The painting depicted blonde headed men who all looked alike. They jumped and ran through the night, in all directions with their arms up, reaching for the exaggerated stars in the sky. Among all the moving bodies were dogs who ran and jumped in between the blonde-headed men. The colors were dark blues, purples, bright yellows, and greens. A pale and translucent white moonlight illuminated everything. I can still picture the painting in my mind.

Doug explained the painting to me. "The men depict our aspirations to the stars while being hindered by well-meaning, loving, and affectionate thoughts, disguised as dogs."

I love the memory of the painting and haven't seen Doug in thirty years. I don't know where he is, what he is doing, and still, consider him to be one of my best friends. We have done only what we could. We've continued on.

I last saw Moses playing guitar in New Orleans. His band was playing a small club I stumbled into. We found a seat at a small table, after his first set.

"Man, I left the Illinois-Iowa Border when I was nineteen years old," he said, not smiling, not hiding anything, just saying it. "I was looking to make a mark, wasn't going back home until I did," he said.

I leaned forward. "And when you went back?" I asked over the surrounding noise.

He took a drink and scanned the room, looking for his band. "Never went back," he said.

"Why?" I asked.

He thought for a moment and smiled contently. "I guess, after a while, it just didn't make sense anymore. It didn't matter."

He stood up. I did too.

"I'm taking off, man," Moses announced, "Belize."

"Belize?" I replied, somewhat stunned.

"Yeah," he said coolly. "I got a little thing going on." He gave me his familiar look, smiled, and extended his hand. "I got to get back," he said, looking toward the stage.

I replied with my own smile, and we shook hands. "So you're doing me like that again?" I asked.

"I'm going home, brother," he confessed. Our handshake turned to a hug.

I will miss Moses. He's leaving for a place he has only been to twice and already calls it home. I can see him now, smiling and feeling clean. God speed, Moses. Continue on.

Years ago, when my own children were young, Mrs. Hull would walk her two small dogs by our small house on the cul-de-sac. She would visit with the kids when they were outside. A friendly relationship developed between our family and the Hull's, the retired couple down the street.

Mrs. Hull was kind, the perfect counterbalance to Mr. Hull's rough exterior. She happily described her husband as "an old dog that growled but never bit."

He was a craftsman. His favorite creations, beside his homemade wooden boat, were the dollhouses he made. They were as much folk art as they were dollhouses. The tiny rooms had wallpaper, hardwood floors, area rugs, and even trim around the small windows. The dollhouses had stuccoing, baseboard trim, tint stonework, and other small surprises. He spared no details.

Things normally went as they do in suburbia until the spring day when police cars lined the street. Mr. Hull had been stabbed in his home and news spread that it was his adult son who stabbed him. To me, the incident was a private matter. I never asked questions. Neighbors brought over meals. I kept my distance and was updated by Mrs. Hull.

In the early fall of that year, I came across a huge dollhouse that was started but never completed. The dollhouse was attached to a large piece of plywood that was three-quarters of an inch thick. The framing and exterior walls were complete. The roof, made from tiny pieces of cedar, was started but not finished. The size of the dollhouse and the work already done was impressive.

"I found it in my attic and just need it out, ten dollars, and it's yours," the owner informed me as he crossed his arms. With an additional ten dollars in his pocket, he helped me slide the dollhouse into the back of my truck.

All the way over, I imagined how thrilled he would be with this magnificent, half-finished, dollhouse. I felt good about myself as I backed into Mr. Hull's driveway, unannounced.

Mr. Hull came out of his front door as I backed the truck up to his driveway to his carport. He didn't approach the truck. He stood still near his front door.

"What do you have there?" he yelled to me as I opened the door of the truck to get out.

"Oh, I don't know, " I answered. "I just ran across this old thing, and I thought you might be able to do something with it." I felt proud, as I said it.

His feet remained planted. "It's big," he said without enthusiasm.

Something wasn't right suddenly.

I studied his reactions. Unsure of the situation, I spoke with caution. "Well, I thought maybe," I hesitated. "You could um, use it?" My statement became a question as I spoke.

He walked to the side of the truck. His left arm was across his stomach, and the elbow of his right arm rested on his left. He rubbed his chin with his right hand as he thought. "I haven't worked on a dollhouse, well, to be honest, I haven't been-" he stammered, and his eyes started to well up. He looked down and continued his thought. "I was in the room where I worked on my dollhouses when my son stabbed me."

It stunned me, and I stood silently as he continued.

"I haven't been in that room since," he said.

For a few moments, we shared the same awkward space.

"Well," I let out, not wanting him to feel pressed. "At the least, you have some firewood." He said nothing. The incomplete dollhouse felt like an anchor within a matter of minutes. All I wanted to do was say the right thing. I attempted, "It's not a big deal at all. I could -"

"Leave it here," he interrupted.

"Are you sure?" I asked, hoping he wouldn't change his mind.

"Yeah, what the hell," he said like it was nothing.

We slid the dollhouse out of the bed of my truck, and I left feeling unresolved and awkward. Not another word was said about the dollhouse when I occasionally saw Mr. Hull. I assumed it became firewood.

That Christmas Eve Mrs. Hull called to ask for my help to move a few boxes at their home. When I arrived, Mr. Hull met me at the door.

"Over here," he motioned. I followed him to a corner in his dining room, where he pointed to an old stucco dollhouse. It looked like a farmhouse. It had two floors, a red roof, a front porch, six rooms, and was open from the back. The rooms had wallpaper, hardwood floors, tiny molding, and a fireplace. The dollhouse was incredibly detailed, an obvious labor of love. "I'd like you to give this to your daughter," he said, as I stood, unable to speak or move.

I spoke up. "I will tell her exactly where it came from," I said with devotion and loyalty. It choked me up.

"No," he scoffed, "follow me." He leads me into his back room, where I saw the most spectacular dollhouse I have ever seen—to this day.

"It's going to the Children's Hospital," he said, looking the dollhouse over. "It's the one you brought over."

When I remember that tremendous dollhouse, I think of all the children who have played with it and who will play with it. I feel things continuing on all around me.

Sometimes a thought or an idea wanders the streets for days, weeks, or years. Sometimes thoughts and ideas are so clear and so urgent that upon the first meeting, they sweep you off your feet and within minutes, they're sitting at your kitchen table. I've come to better like the ones who have been wandering. They're much more polite and have more experience. They are poised, more steadfast, and in the end, more helpful.

You can walk with them or have them at your table. Either way, with you or without you, they will only do what they know – continue on.

Two Points on a Continuum

1975 - Talbot County, Maryland

Boat only left his prison cell when it was mandatory. Still, in shock, he spent days in his bed. Most of the time, he pulled his sheet over himself.

Kin went to Boat. Once Boat talked to Kin, everything came out - his life, his friends, Hope, Jessie's death, his fears and his thoughts of, maybe just ending it all.

"Trouble follows you like a loyal dog. You need to learn how to train that dog," Kin advised.

"That's how you see it?" Boat asked.

"There's more, but that's the gist of it," Kin grunted and leaned forward in his chair, facing Boat. "It's for you to figure. You fill in the blanks, not me."

"I don't think I know how," Boat admitted aloud.

"One step at a time," Kin said, getting up to leave. "You do your part. Stop hiding in your bunk, and I'll do mine." Not knowing what to say, Boat sat in silence and watched Kin walk out of his cell.

Sam Peel was a lifer who was charged with three murders outside of prison and suspected of a few more inside. Peel, as he was known in prison, had a coldness that could be felt from a distance; it ran deep. He stood five foot six and weighed a hundred and forty pounds. His hair was grey, short, and shaved close on the sides. His eyes were bright blue. His face was pockmarked, and his arms, shoulders, and chest were covered with jailhouse tattoos.

Every violent act he had committed or was committed on his behalf was done swiftly and surgically. Every act was rationalized and controlled. There were never emotional outbursts from Peel or his group.

"When something needs to get done, it gets done," Peel explained to Kin after a man was beaten to death in the prison pantry. "No need to talk about it," Peel advised. Peel had control of the prison population. His circle of associates was intensely loyal as it was their loyalty that assured their safety. Through the prison, it was understood that you could do what you wanted as long as it didn't affect Peel or go against his understood code of conduct.

Understanding the prison chain of command early on, Kin visited Peel's mother. He wore his collar and sometimes brought groceries. With each visit, Kin would bring a good word about or from Peel. He told her he spoke to Peel about salvation, words she needed to hear in her old age.

Giving an old woman, a killer's mother, a sense of redemption for her son didn't buy salvation; it bought loyalty.

Soon after meeting Boat, Kin went to Peel while he was outside in the prison yard. "I need an eye kept on the kid," Kin said. Peel took the last drag of his cigarette, dropped it, and twisted it into the ground with his shoe and exhaled smoke.

"He's a good kid," Kin insisted, moving closer to Peel.

"Done," Peel decided. "Consider it done," he said and walked away without another word.

Weeks later, Boat pulled Kin to the side after a group counseling session. "How can I become more steady," he asked quietly, not wanting anyone else to hear.

Two days later, Kin stopped by Boat's cell. "Here you are," Kin said and set down a small stack of books; the Bible, Viktor Frankl's Man's Search for Meaning, the Urantia Book, Jack Kerouac's, Dharma Bums, and Sal's, Tzu, Freelance Philosopher, Ancestor of the Divine. "Start by reading these," Kin said dryly. "Take care of them, they're mine, and I'll want them back." From that point, Boat read, drew, and painted.

Boat received random visits from his friends. His Mother and Hope visited every two weeks, always together. Hope was pregnant. She began to show shortly after she started visiting and refused to discuss who the baby's father was. Sometimes, Raymond tagged along with them. Overall, Raymond visited the most, always with a laugh and a smile.

Kin and Boat spent more and more time together. Kin loved telling stories of his past, and Boat loved listening to them. While Kin reminisced and shared ideas, Boat would draw and paint. Kin shared more with Boat than anyone, save Sal.

"You can read people by the lines in their face," Kin explained to Boat. "The lines in a person's face show what life has etched into them. Look at how a person's eyes are shaped, how they sit, the lines on their forehead, on the sides of their eyes, around their mouth." Kin stopped. "I'm serious." He started again. "I can see how much someone smiles, how much they worry, years of pain, joy- it's not bullshit."

"I'm listening," Boat replied, as he sketched a portrait of Kin without him realizing.

Kin continued out loud with his thoughts. "You can feel a person by studying those lines," looking around at the examples around him as he spoke. "How they walk. How they speak. How they look at you." Kin stopped and turned to Boat. "I know them before they speak a word."

Boat continued to draw, paint, and read. One day, Kin, for the first time, looked through Boat's drawings and paintings. He didn't say a word as he looked long and hard at each picture. Two days later, Kin walked Boat out to his drawing area. "This was all donated by some school," he said, pointing to sheets of thick drawing paper, colored pencils, paints, and an easel.

Boat knew Kin bought the supplies. In silent appreciation, Boat sketched colored pencil portraits of Caroline's sister's children, who now called Caroline Mom. He sketched the images from photographs Caroline had sent Kin.

"Jesus," Kin said without thinking when Boat presented him with the finished portraits. "They look like photographs." He gushed in amazement as he sat in a chair and examined the portraits. "Jesus Christ," he repeated over and over. Kin sent the sketches to Caroline, who had them framed and hung them over her fireplace mantel.

Boat used acrylics to paint abstracts. "I lie down and close my eyes until I see colors in my mind," he said, trying to explain the process to Kin. "I try to replicate the colors on the canvas before they leave my mind. The toughest part is that the colors constantly move around."

Manuel Acuno, a Central American, doing six months for assault, was the first to comment on Boat's abstract paintings. "Alto arte," he said as he walked by Boat's art area.

Surprised to hear the first words he had ever heard Manuel speak, Boat turned as Manual continued walking. "I'm sorry, what?" Boat asked.

Manual stopped, looked over at Boat's painting, and pointed. "High-art amigo, Alto arte."

Time went by. A few of the inmates became close friends with Boat. The most notable was an ex-marine who went by the name JWC. He was Peel's most feared enforcer and was assigned Boat's safety, a fact Boat was oblivious to. Whenever Boat painted or sketched and Kin wasn't around, JWC was sharing his philosophies, codes of survival or watching his back from a distance.

Kin continued to work between the two the prisons he served. He met with inmates, wrote sermons, and facilitated group meetings. He watched inmates leave and watched as many returned. He corresponded with Sal, Caroline, and his brother Michael through letters. Occasionally, he would get a phone call from one of his children.

Over time, his initial idea of saving souls gave way to the stark reality he was trading time for money. "Spirituality does not grow on concrete floors. It takes root and grows in your mind," Kin evangelized. Unfortunately, there was only a small percentage that could comprehend such ideas and an even smaller percentage who take those ideas and change their thoughts and actions.

After nineteen months, Boat was being moved to a halfway house to begin his transition to society. "Look me up when you're free and clear," Kin told Boat the day he left for the halfway house.

Two weeks after Boat was sent to the half-way house, Sal Atwater, the Tzu, The Ancestor of the divine, Evie's husband, Father, and Kin's lifelong friend, passed away. They found him in the early morning, in his hammock along the sea of Cortez.

Kin left a message with Mark Herald, his supervisor, and immediately left for Mexico. He was in San Felipe within thirty hours of getting the news, determined to preside over Sal's service.

"Sal was too bold, too colorful, too alive to just quietly go as he did," Evie said as she embraced Kin, forcing a smile as she spoke.

Kin stayed in the same hut Sal had prepared for him a few years earlier. Two days later, Kin presided over Sal's sunrise memorial service along the sea of Cortez. Of the over two hundred people that showed up for Sal's service, Kin only knew his wife, Evie.

"There's something beautiful in finding something, someone," Kin said, beginning Sal's service. "But, maybe, more beautiful, is being found." He paused. "Though I will miss my friend, it comforts me to know that he's been found, permanently." Kin looked out at the assembled group and the sea behind them. He spoke of the fruits of Sal's labors, his love for life, the sea, and his creative pursuits. "All of what Sal had ever done, or what he became was brought about by his love and concern for people," Kin shared. He looked over the crowd and noticed the tear-stained faces of people he had never met. Words came to Kin in a flash. He repeated them on impulse, barely hearing the words he spoke. "Sal always had redemption," Kin said. "He just never knew what it felt like." He let his mind catch up. "So, he took it on. He became a redeemer." Kin turned to Evie. "He never could leave well enough alone," he said with a smile.

Over the next few days, Kin met most of Sal's visiting friends, associates, and opportunists who all claimed to be a close friend of Sal's.

Evie, always the pragmatic one, was with Sal's publisher when Kin came to say goodbye. "Business still needs to be attended to," Evie said as she walked toward Kin. Under a thatched gazebo roof, Evie embraced Kin. She pulled back to look at him squarely. "You are always welcome. You know that, don't you?"

Mi casa es su casa, he thought to himself. " I'll always remember," he responded. He hugged Evie and left San Felipe.

Back in Maryland, Kin's insides felt tight. He held his breath at times for no reason. His body nervously shook. He could not concentrate on a single thought for more than a few seconds. Cascades of half-formed thoughts bombarded his mind. Pieces of pictures and perceived failures, every mistake he ever made, every misstep, his failed marriage, relationships with his children, his unforgivable sin in England - everything, real and unreal, tossed him violently into the rocks. This is not the time to shed a tear, he thought, trying to steady himself, this is the time to survive, to continue on. He became quieter, harder.

What Kin deemed his only effective medicine lived in bottles. He abandoned wine for whiskey, peace for numbness. Kin's drinking spilled into the day, giving him a jump on the evil stillness that waited for him each night.

Though many witnessed a change in Kin, it was only Bobby Davis, a corrections officer who worked the first shift who was bold enough to confront Kin.

Kin sat alone in the break room, finishing up an early lunch when Bobby walked in. "Kin, have a second?" he asked.

"Sure, Bobby," Kin responded, never looking up as he finished his sandwich.

Bobby leaned back against the counter. His nightstick tapped the cabinet door. "I just wanted to say, well, I thought, I mean, I was thinking," he leaned forward, took a breath and let his words roll downhill. "I wanted to see if you were ok," he blurted out.

"Oh," is all Kin said in response as he cleaned up his lunch and stood up. "I'm good, thanks, Bobby."

Bobby looked down at his feet and leaned back against the counter. His nightstick, again, tapped the cabinet door. He lifted his hand and scratched the back of his head. "Well see, the things is-"

"I already answered your question, Bobby," Kin interrupted, tossing his trash in the wastebasket and walking towards the break room door. Bobby made bold and took a step, positioning himself between Kin and the door. "Kin if you could just-"

Kin was inches from Bobby's face when he cut him off in mid-sentence. "Bobby, I'm going to give you a few seconds to move." His words were deliberate and dry as dust. His eyes locked on Bobby's. Bobby looked down, cleared his throat, and moved to the side without saying a word. Kin said nothing and walked to the door. He stopped and looked out the small window of the break room door. "I appreciate your concern, thank you," he said, looking out the small window. Kin opened the door and walked out of the break room.

While Kin was on his own and spiraling, Boat excelled, inspired by Kin. Boat was assigned a day job working in a warehouse that shipped out tractor parts and farm equipment. Each night, he returned to the group home where he read, ate, and painted with supplies that had been dropped off by Hope. She dropped off two boxes of brushes, paints, boards, and canvases. Inside a box, she left a one-word note - Always. Boat only needed that one word.

Boat continued to develop his practice of meditative painting. He would prep his painting area, prepare the canvas, and make sure his paints were all set up. He would then sit and read inspirational material, followed by silence and meditation. He concentrated on his breathing and waited until all the thoughts in his mind got quiet. When it felt right, he went to his easel and started to paint. Sometimes the music was on, and sometimes it never occurred to him to put it on. He painted without expectation.

"It's the cleanest high I've ever felt," he said, trying his best to explain it to Hope. "It doesn't happen a lot, but when it does, I feel like I'm outside my body."

On the day Boat left the halfway house, he carefully placed all of his painting supplies in one of the two boxes they arrived in. He needed two more large boxes to hold the carefully wrapped paintings he had painted while there.

The parole officer arrived and helped him fill out the required paperwork. "Six months parole with time served," he informed Boat as he folded the papers and placed them in a state labeled envelope. "Stay out of trouble," the parole officer offered as they shook hands.

"Yes, sir," Boat replied.

Trembling with excitement, Boat gathered all of his belongings and waited on the front stoop of the halfway house, a free man, save his parole time. Minutes later, Hope, Raymond and Hope's son, Levon, who was just over fifteen months, arrived in Boat's car.

"Yes!" Boat screamed out when he saw them pull up in his car. "Right on," he yelled when Raymond popped out of the driver's seat. "Now, that's the last time you drive my car," Boat said, laughing and pointing to Raymond. He walked around the front of the car to meet Hope. As Hope climbed from the passenger side, he grabbed her hands and stood her up.

"How you doing?" he asked with a warm smile and hugged her tightly, lifting her off her feet. "I loved your note," he said, pulled back, gave her a good look and a kiss.

Hope turned back to the car. "And," she said, pulling Levon from the car. "Levon," she announced as she eased him to the ground.

"Well hello Levon," Boat said, trying to shake his hand gently, "I'm Boat."

Hope lifted Levon to her hip. "Hello Boat," she said for Levon as he shyly looked at Boat.

The subject of who Levon's father remained an off-limits conversation. Hope refused to discuss it with anyone. Boat studied Levon's face, looking for traces of himself.

Within minutes, Boat's art supplies and paintings were in the trunk, and he was behind the wheel of his car. Raymond was in the back next to Levon and Hope was in the front.

The first stop was Sanders Soul Food Kitchen that served breakfast all day. Raymond insisted on buying Boat his first meal, an omelet, and pancakes. "It's not the last supper, more like the first breakfast," Raymond yelled out, laughing hardest at his own joke. The conversation started loud and jovial and slowly turned quieter.

"If it's ok," Boat announced while finishing the last of his pancakes. "I have a few things I need to do. Can we catch up later?" he asked.

"Yes sir," he said excitedly, smacking his hand down on the table. "But remember, you have a little thing later" Customers turned to look from his sudden noise. "People who want to see you, make sure you are back by seven," he said without noticing the commotion he caused.

"I'm not going," Hope announced, wetting a napkin to clean pancake syrup off Levon. "I'm not leaving Levon to go to one of your parties, Raymond."

"Hope," Raymond replied, "it's Butter, when are you going to call me Butter?"

Boat looked at Hope and then to Raymond. "How about we drop you off first," he suggested.

"Let's go, Captain!" Raymond yelled out and jumped up from his seat. Levon giggled watching Raymond.

Boat dropped Raymond off at his house, where Boat had agreed to stay. They unloaded Boat's art supplies and brought them into the house while Hope and Levon waited in the car.

As Boat was about to leave, Raymond stopped him on the porch. "Seven o'clock, my man," he reminded Boat, grabbing his arm, "welcome home party."

"Hell yeah," Boat shot back, and they slapped their hands together.

As Boat started down the stairs, Raymond called out, "Hey Boat."

Boat stopped, "Yeah?" he answered, turning around.

"Don't mind her," Raymond replied in a quiet voice. "She's been nervous as hell waiting for you."

"Thanks, man," Boat said, turned and darted to his car.

"So what do you have to do?" Hope asked, staring out her window, watching the trees fly by as Boat drove to her house.

"I need to go see Reverend Kin, the guy I told you about," Boat replied. "I know you remember me talking about him." He looked over to see Hope still staring out the window.

"I see," she replied without expression.

He looked over to her again as he drove. "You ok?"

"Yeah," she said, holding her gaze out the window.

"Look at me, Hope," Boat insisted.

"What?" she said, turning to him.

"Are you ok?"

"Of course I am, Boat," she replied with a tight smile.

At her parents' house, Boat was not sure what to say. All he could think about was seeing Kin again. He walked around to the passenger side and helped Hope with the car seat.

He walked up close to her. "Let me do this, ok?" he asked.

"Sure," she said with Levon on her hip. She turned and walked toward her house.

"Just me and you later," Boat yelled as she walked up to the stairs to the front porch.

"Ok Boat," she yelled back, never turning around.

Boat arrived at the prison to find Kin had called out sick. With directions in hand, Boat headed to the small town where Kin lived. He was anxious and imagined how happy Kin would be to see him.

He pushed the gas pedal to the floor and held his left arm out the window to cut the air. The wind blew in his face as he sped over country roads. Music from the radio overtook the noise of the wind and the engine. Naaa naaa - na na na na - na na na na - Hey Jude! Boat wanted to feel that way forever.

It was just before dinner when Boat found Kin's house, a small ranch with a front porch and a low roof. It sat close to the road and was a block away from the bay. An unkempt garden full of weeds, tomatoes, peppers, carrots, marigolds, sunflowers, and an azalea filled the shallow front yard that sat behind a chain-link fence. A flagstone path that led to the front porch split the garden.

Boat parked just past the house. He heard music playing from inside, Townes Van Zandt. An old Basset hound that saw Boat from inside the house barked and pushed the screen door open. The hound slowly meandered to the fence and wagged her tail, giving out an occasional bark. "Tink!" Kin yelled from inside the house.

Kin pushed the screen door open and saw Boat outside the fence. Standing with the door half open, Kin squinted and rubbed his eyes in the afternoon sun. "Boat?" he asked.

"Reverend Kin," Boat yelled back as the old dog jumped up on the fence to get more attention.

Kin stepped back into the house. "Do you need anything?" he asked from behind his screen door.

That day, Kin had slept until the early afternoon, hung over from the night before. His thoughts had been more and more on Caroline. He desperately wanted to reach out but was ashamed of how he was, scared of being rejected.

Boat stood up straight behind the chain-linked fence and yelled to Kin, "I just came by to-"

"Hold on now Boat, I'll be right back," Kin interrupted. He went back into the house to straighten up the living room and kitchen. He moved bottles of Vodka and Jim Beam under the sink and put a button-up shirt on over his t-shirt. He ran water from the kitchen faucet, rinsed his face, dried it off with a dishrag, walked back to the front door, and pushed the screen door open. "Come on in," he yelled out, "she won't bite." Tink followed Boat to the front porch, wagging her tail and giving an occasional bark.

"Good to see you," Kin said, shaking Boat's hand, greeting him at the door. He motioned Boat through a small living room to a large table that sat closer to the kitchen. The dog followed the men to the table. "Her name is Tinkerbell," Kin said, petting the old Bassett. "A family down the street had to move and couldn't keep her. I call her Tink." He took a seat, inviting Boat to sit across from him.

The breakfast area they sat in was next to the kitchen. Boat sat down at the table and quickly scanned the sparsely decorated living room. To the back, French doors faced the backyard. Through the French doors, Boat could see another unkempt garden.

"I'm planning on moving," Kin said. "That's why the place looks this way."

"What?" Boat replied, confused by Kin's statement.

"I might move," Kin spoke up. "That's why things look the way they do."

"Oh, ok." Boat responded, "Where to?" he asked.

"Who knows," Kin replied, shrugging the question off. He stood up and walked toward the refrigerator. "Would you like some iced tea?"

"I'm good," Boat replied, petting Tink, "thanks though."

"Suit yourself," Kin muttered as he brought back a glass and pitcher of iced tea. "Why are you here?" he asked as he poured, "I wasn't expecting any company."

Boat leaned back in his seat, smiled, stretched his arms out, and clasped his hands behind his head. "I need nothing. I just wanted to thank you."

"For?" Kin asked, unimpressed.

"For showing me the way Rev." Boat leaned forward and smiled, waiting for Kin's approval.

"What way?" Kin asked deadpanned.

Boat said nothing.

"Don't thank me for anything," Kin scoffed.

Boat was stunned. He noticed a Bible at the end of the table, grabbed it and thumbed through pages. He found a passage and stopped. "Kin it says right here-"

"Put it down!" Kin demanded. His voice was sharp and hoarse.

Boat stopped, looked at Kin, closed the Bible, and placed it between them on the table. Kin looked at Boat and swiped the bible off the table with his arm. The Bible flew through the air and crashed against the wall where it helplessly fell to the ground. It rested on the floor, crumpled. Pages were folded in all ways under the cover. Both men stared at the Bible on the floor in silence.

"Don't come in my house and preach to me," Kin hissed. "And, before you get too full of yourself, live a few years, go through some real shit, and then you can come back and preach all you want."

Boat had no words, and Kin didn't give him a chance. "Do you have something more to say?" Kin asked. Boat said nothing. He stood up and looked down at the Bible on the floor.

"I don't need a parrot," Kin yelled out, finishing his tirade.

Boat felt numb as he walked to the screen door. At the door, he turned to Kin, who was still seated at the table. "If your goal is to be an angry drunk-" he stopped before he said anymore, pushed the screen door open and walked out. The screen door slammed shut and bounced against the doorframe as Boat walked across the porch.

Kin sat at the kitchen table and listened as Boat closed the front gate, opened his car door, started the engine, and pulled away.

Boat drove eighty miles an hour over lazy country roads again, no radio, no songs, no feeling good. He was lost in thought. His mind focused on the sound of the engine, the acceleration, and de-acceleration. He had both hands on the wheel as he squealed around the curves of the road. He drove around for another two hours.

When he finally arrived back at Raymond's, he was an hour late for his own party and didn't notice the cars parked up and down the street. Almost all of Boat's friends and people he didn't know were there. The Haas brothers, who were now in a band, had set their instruments up in one bedroom. His childhood friends, Peachy, Jane, Raymond, Phil, Victoria, Jake, and Collins, the psychedelic tipster, were all there. Boat was on the front porch and lost in thought when he remembered the party was for him. A group of people filed past him on the porch. They were friends of the band and had no idea who he was. Boat followed them in and was greeted with a chorus of "Boat, Boat, Boat," led by Raymond, who was waiting for him in the living room. All who knew Boat came to the living room to shake his hand or give a hug.

Past the living room, to the right, were two bedrooms and a bathroom. Two kegs and snacks were in the first bedroom. They set the band up in the second, cramped but happy. In that room, an old disco ball hung from the ceiling and reflected yellow light from a stolen road construction flasher. A few people sat on the floor. They listened to the band with their eyes closed and backs to the wall.

Back through the dining room, towards the back of the house, Collins was holding court at the big kitchen table. "Do you even understand relativity?" Collins yelled over the music. "You know, rest and motion," he asked, "are they relative or absolute?" he quizzed those at the table. "Does anyone know anything?"

When Collins saw Boat in the entry to the kitchen, he stopped, stood up and held up a cup of beer to toast Boat. "My man Boat, the one with the seven, seven, sevens!" he announced to all around.

"Collins," Boat replied excitedly as they reached over the table and shook hands.

"I'd come around the table and hug you," Collins said with a devilish smile, "but I'm not." Everyone around the table laughed. Collins pointed to a teenager that was closest to Boat. "Go get yourself a chair. That one is now Boat's," he ordered.

Within a few minutes, Boat was sitting among old friends, just as he did before he went into prison.

"What's the topic?" Boat asked over the music, accepting a plastic cup of beer that had been handed to him.

"Well, let's see," Collins mused, "String theory, God, reincarnation, and oh yeah, Mom upside down is wow."

"What?" Boat asked, spitting beer out of his mouth laughing.

"Yeah." Collins smiled and explained over the laughter. "Little Jimmy here," he said, taunting one of the younger ones at the table, "got high and used compound to write WOW on his car hood." More laughter broke out. Jimmy was noticeably embarrassed as Collins continued. "However, when the car drives towards you, it says Mom." The entire table erupted in laughter. A few nudged Jimmy as they laughed.

"Hey, fuck you," was all Jimmy could say as everyone at the table found it hard to not laugh.

"Come on, just stop all that now," Boat scolded the group in a serious tone. He looked over at Jimmy, who seemed pleased to finally have some support. The table got quiet. "Now Jimmy," Boat inquired, "did you mean, wow mom, or mom wow?" The table again burst into laughter at the joke that refused to die. Jimmy repeated, "Fuck you." Girls in the kitchen laughed and put their arms around Jimmy from behind. "We still love you," they assured him.

The laughter died down, and the discussions flowed back to politics, philosophy, and religion. "There is shit we know," Collins yelled out, moving his hands in the air as he spoke.

"Science is observation. How do you derive absolutes from secular observations?" Boat asked. "Things that look a certain way might just be part of bigger things, with different rules," It was what he and Collins did. It was like he had never left.

Tracy Marie Kempski had been making eye contact with Boat all night. She was a few years younger and not a part of Boat's direct group of friends - but she knew of him and despised Hope. Rumors circulated about Tracy, rumors that didn't bother her at all.

Shortly after midnight, Boat was still at the kitchen table, trying to erase his confrontation with Kin. Tracy caught Boat's attention from the living room and waved for him to come over. Without a word, Boat got up from the table and went to her. As he walked toward her, she opened the door that led to the attic. He followed her and closed the door behind them. He followed her up the stairs, through a small storage area, and through another door that opened to a small dark room. The room had angled ceilings, a window, a chair, and a table.

When he entered the room, she was standing in front of the only window in the small room. Her back was to him. Light from the outside streetlamp made her a perfect silhouette. He walked toward her. She turned around and, without saying a word, pushed him back onto the chair in the middle of the room. She stood in front of him and rubbed her hands through his hair and over his shoulders. He closed his eyes, and she placed her finger under his chin, lifting his head up to look at her. When Boat opened his eyes, she started to caress her chest, looking down at him. She stopped and took a few steps back. Light from the street lamp outside touched her body. She was curves and shadows. In silence, she pulled her shirt above her head and caressed her bare breasts. "Do you like me?" she asked.

She stepped toward Boat and pulled his head to her chest. Her back arched as Boat clumsily grabbed at her hips. He pulled her closer, breathing heavily as he kissed her breasts. She moved her hands to Boat's shoulders and pushed herself away, out of his reach. She stepped back again, no words, only breathing. After a moment, she moved to Boat, knelt down and pulled his shorts and boxers down to his ankles. She looked up and teased him. "I want you ready for me," she whispered.

She stood up, magically undressed, and twirled her hair with her finger. Boat reached forward, grabbed her hips, and pulled her down on him. She grabbed his shoulders and pushed his head against her chest. She arched her back, moved forward, and leaned back again. Her hands grabbed his hair. She moved her hips back and forth, grinding him faster. Within minutes, it was over.

Boat sat, stunned. He watched her put her clothes on as he caught his breath. Once dressed, she smiled, bit her lower lip, giggled, left the room, and closed the door behind her. After what seemed like a few minutes, Boat pulled up his shorts and headed downstairs. He felt like he was fifteen minutes behind everything that was going on around him. By the time he made it back downstairs, Raymond had passed out, and most of the people had already left, including Tracy. Only the drunk remained.

Boat walked outside to a dying fire pit. He sat and drank two more beers and watched the embers. He felt drunk and alone, and did the only thing he knew to do.

At her open window, at the back corner of the house, he whispered for her, "Hope."

Hope had just hung up the phone and was lying in her bed, in the dark, awake. She stared at him without saying a word. Boat saw she was awake and pointed toward the hammock in the backyard where they had spent many hours over the years. Within a few minutes, Hope came through the back door to the hammock.

"What are you doing here, David James, what do you want?" she asked impatiently. "You have no right to come here in the middle of the night. Things have changed David. I have a son now!"

Boat sat at the edge of the hammock and extended his hand, "I know. I'm wrong." She turned away from him, crossed her arms, and shook her head. "I don't even know why I do this," she said as she walked around to the other side of the hammock like she had a hundred times before. "Just for a few minutes and you better be out of here by morning," she said as they laid down and she leaned back against him. She felt him bury his head into her back and squeeze her tight. "I know what you did with Tracy. She's already told half the town," Hope seethed.

Boat said nothing. She crossed her arms in front of her. "Nothing to say?" she asked.

"I messed up, that's not who I am," was all he could get out.

"That's what you did. Don't tell me it's not who you are. Maybe that's exactly who you are." Her words cut deep.

"Levon is not your Son," she said without emotion.

"Ok," he said in a low whisper as he continued to squeeze her tight and bury his head against her. She felt the heat from his tears against the back of her neck.

"Damn you, David," she let out, reached back and punched his leg.

Sometime during the night, decisions were made in Boat's mind, maybe while he slept. Boat knew he was changed.

Early in the morning, Hope came out and woke Boat. Hope's parents had made breakfast and asked Hope to bring him in. During breakfast, Hope noticed Boat occasionally wipe tears away, trying to conceal it.

A few months later, Boat was painting in Raymond's dining room they had converted into a small painting studio. He heard a knock at the front screen door and walked around the corner to a shadow in the doorway he instantly recognized.

"Rev Kin, what are you doing here?" he asked.

"Hey, Boat," Kin replied sheepishly.

Boat pushed the door open with his foot. "I'm covered in paint," Boat said, holding up his paint-splattered hands. "Come on in, I'm about finished mixing." He headed back toward his makeshift studio, pushing aside the hanging beads that separated the dining room and living room. "Hold on," he said, holding up a finger.

He took the needle off Dylan's, Blonde on Blonde and finished mixing green and blue on his palette.

Kin said nothing as he walked into the makeshift studio. He scanned the living room, kitchen, and studio area. A large drop cloth covered the wood floor. The exterior wall was mostly windows. The rest of the dining room was open to the house and separated by the hanging beads.

"Sometimes, I'll paint something at night, and it'll look different in the day," Boat said as they stood in the sunlight filled room.

"I see," was all Kin said, looking over the paintings in various stages of completion.

"These are all yours?" Kin asked while he studied the paintings.

Boat followed Kin's gaze. "Well yeah, they-"

"May I?" Kin interrupted. "May I hold it?" he asked as he bent over one of Boat's spiritual abstracts.

"Um, yeah sure," Boat answered.

Kin picked up the painting and held his arms out straight. "What do you call this?" he asked, staring at the picture.

Boat looked nervously at the ground. "See her Shine," he replied. He answered like he was revealing a secret.

"See her Shine?" Kin asked.

"Yes," Boat said contently.

Kin walked sideways through the beads and set the painting against a console that was five feet from the couch. He sat on the couch and stared at the painting. "Jesus Christ," he said to himself quietly. "This is beautiful." Kin proclaimed. "I have never seen anything like this before." Kin looked down and rubbed his eyes. His face became red. "I don't know," he continued, "I can't get over it. I don't think I've ever seen a painting that held so much. I think I can feel this damn thing," he said. Kin stood up, still looking at the painting. "See her Shine," he announced.

"See her Shine," Boat repeated.

"How the hell do you do something like that?" Kin asked.

"It's crazy," Boat replied. "I just meditate. When I feel it, I start to paint."

"Feel it," Kin asked.

"Yeah," Boat replied.

"Prayer?" Kin asked.

"I don't know," Boat answered, "maybe worship." He thought for a moment, "It's a tough place to get to."

"Tell me about it," Kin replied. "Damn," Kin said aloud as he looked back to the painting again, "See her Shine."

When he looked back to Boat, his expression changed. "I left my job," he informed Boat. "I'm going to Texas for a spell. "

"That woman, your friend?" Boat asked, remembering Caroline. "Hold on, let me wash my hands," he said, holding his hands up. "I need to get the paint off before it dries."

When Boat returned from the kitchen, he noticed a book sitting on a corner of a table. "What's this?" he asked.

"See for yourself," Kin replied, smiling.

Boat grabbed the hard-covered book. "Two Points on a Continuum," he said excitedly. He turned the book over and looked at the back cover without opening it. "Wow," he said with emotion, "for me?" he asked.

"Open the cover," Kin urged.

Boat opened the hard book cover to see Sal's handwriting.

"To the man who knows the man. Take a breath; it's only part of a continuum. All the best, Sal. "

"Sal passed away a little while ago," Kin announced as Boat scanned the book. "I told him about you when he was alive. I had hoped you would have met him."

Boat closed the book and looked at Kin. "I am sorry Kin. I know he meant-"

Don't be." Kin interrupted, "he had a good run."

"I'll treasure it," Boat declared as he held the book, caressing it.

"I have something else," Kin said, looking at Boat seriously. "I'm leaving in a few weeks. I've already paid my rent in advance for the year. I have ten months left and thought it might be a place you can stay until you figure your next move. You'd have to get the utilities changed to your name."

Boat plopped down on the couch. "Are you serious, why?" Boat asked. "I need to figure this out," he said, clearing his throat. "I don't know what to say."

"Don't say anything," Kin insisted and handed Boat a piece of paper. "My cousin Betty Anne has a daughter who runs an art gallery in England. I told them about you and your art. They're expecting to hear from you." He tapped the paper with his finger as he spoke. "Their address and phone numbers are on the paper. I told them you would contact them and send pictures of your work."

"What?" Boat asked and leaned back in disbelief. "This is too much to handle."

Life paths were changing, and still, there was Sal, reminding them both to not get too caught up. After all, it's just two points on a continuum.

The Man Named Boat

It was Easter morning when I woke from a vivid dream, a dream that felt prophetic. Not given to dream interpretation, I still felt that something meaningful had slipped through. The phrase I came away with, the one that immediately struck me, that was inexplicably repeated, over and over in my mind was a stranger in my Father's house.

In this dream, I had entered what I thought was my own father's house. That in itself was unusual as I never had much of a relationship with my own Father and hadn't seen him in many years. In the dream, the house I entered was indescribably large and seemed to unfold and expand once I was inside. It was a mansion of mansions.

I never saw my Father in the dream and the reality he could never afford such a place, or that a place like this could exist, didn't strike me as odd. I wandered from room to room, level by level, as assortments of people filed by, people that neither my Father nor I knew. I felt an overwhelming sadness for my father in the dream. Then, the sadness turned to me. I realized I

197

did not belong in the grand house. I knew it, and the people who passed by and looked at me also knew it.

In the distance, I saw a large party in the courtyard of the mansion. I curled up and laid down in a carpeted hallway, watching it all. Then, a huge oak crashed through the woods and into the courtyard without a sound. There was no calamity, and no one was hurt. The party continued around the toppled Oak. I felt empty when I woke from my dream.

Given it was Easter, I drove to the sleepy water town that has always drawn me. Thoughts of my dream and its possible meanings or non-meanings swirled through my head as I drove.

It was my first visit to this church, and it felt like everyone from the tiny town was there. The congregation all seemed to know each other. They were loose and comfortable. I was not.

Even in my own discomfort, there was a joy that could be felt, and I was glad to be there. I sat in a pew with my arms crossed, scanning the room and studying the people in it. I was content and distant, content to be distant.

The Pastor was a short, pot-bellied ball of white hair, glasses, and beard. He wore a long black robe and exuded happiness, genuine happiness. His eyes sparkled.

After some music and a reading of church events, he started his sermon, reading passages on the resurrection. He described how Jesus overcame death and its significance in our own lives. He emphasized the event as a reason to celebrate. It was exactly what folks expected and wanted for their Easter Service, like a band who played their greatest hits, songs that everyone could sing along with.

He grabbed the sides of the pulpit like a rock in a sea of waves and finished his sermon from the heart. "I sure do appreciate you coming here and want to remind you it's your choice. It's your choice to believe that behind the stone was the one who was resurrected and it's your choice in not only what you believe, but in how you act." He paused for a moment. "It's your choice. All I ask is that you include the Lord in your choices. "His voice rose as he finished. "Amen," he cried out.

"Amen," the congregation returned in happy unison.

The Pastor stepped down from the pulpit. He grabbed a loaf of bread in one hand and a gold goblet in the other. He then walked up and down the center aisle, explaining the meaning of the bread and the wine. He made an effort to look into the eyes of every person in the room as he spoke. "There is a basket up front if you wish to donate after receiving the blood and body of Christ," he reminded the congregation. "So come on up as you would like." His voice was bold and comforting, and made you smile for no reason. With no further instruction, a line formed and slowly started to inch forward. Getting impatient, I looked to see what was holding things up. The delay was because of the Pasto. He leaned against the front pew, greeted and conversed with each and every person as they approached.

As I waited, I drifted to a memory from long ago, also in a church. I remembered watching communion from the first pew of a large and crowded church. A pipe organ played as I watched person after person take the bread dipped in wine, each different face, silently asking in their own way.

Something brought me back to the present as the line crept forward. It was the pastor's voice. "Welcome to my father's house," he said to me. I immediately understood the meaning of my dream.

The weather that day was beautiful. After the service, I walked the two blocks down to the canal. At the canal, I walked along the wooden dock of the small marina. I watched as boaters cleaned their boats, some getting ready for a day on the bay. The sun caressed my winter skin as the water gently lapped against the docked boats. The day convinced me to stop and enjoy a drink.

Minutes later, I found myself on an upper deck of a restaurant with an orange juice and tequila. The historic, upscale restaurant had cedar shake siding on the outside and plaster walls on the inside. It was a place where most could only afford a drink or two.

Directly across the canal and straight ahead was another restaurant along the water. It was sleek and white with dark-tinted windows and had large pots of flowers on an outside deck. To my left was a dirt access road near a grassy hill that followed the canal to the bay. To my right, a wood dock hugged the land. The dock was connected to a dozen floating docks that were eight feet wide and stretched into the canal, creating dozens of boat slips. Ten to twelve small to medium size boats attached to each side. The larger boats were further down, closer to Molly's Restaurant.

As I sat, enjoying the day, my peripheral vision caught something, a flash of light maybe. I turned to the right. In the distance, I saw it, not a light but a reflection. The reflection was from a silver-white head of hair that blew in the wind and shined as bright as Christmas tinsel. There he was, the white-haired Pastor, hurriedly walking down the dock, robe still on and elbows swinging. I focused and watched him enter a large boat at the other end of the dock, shaking a man's hand as he entered the boat.

I became curious, so curious that I started to eat lunch at Molly's, the restaurant that sits across from the large boat the Pastor visited. Each week at 11:15, I took a seat on the outside deck and watch the white-haired Pastor enter the boat. Each visit starts with a handshake. They move to the upper deck of the boat, talk, and have a few drinks. On two occasions, another pastor joined them.

On the fourth Sunday I had been watching, after my lunch, I wandered to the dock to get a closer look at the boat. As I did, I noticed a posted sign toward the rear of the boat. As I approached the sign, the man who owned the boat, the one I had only seen from a distance, walked toward me.

He brought his hand up over his eyes like a hat brim and squinted at the sun behind me. "Can I help you with anything?" he asked.

"I was wondering what this sign is all about," I replied, looking over the boat.

"Like it says, I need some help," he answered and put on a pair of sunglasses.

He was tall, over six feet, lanky but sturdy. He wore a pair of boating shorts, a t-shirt, and sandals. His hair was gray, and his skin was tan. He moved like a younger man. At the same time, he looked like someone who had been washed by the sea.

"I'm assuming you already have a job," he said, looking me over.

"I do," I responded.

"Well, if you know of someone," he said and started to walk by.

As he passed, I blurted out a question. "What are you looking for?" I'm curious about everything, the boat, the sign, and the visits by the white-haired Pastor.

He stopped and turned around. "I need someone to help out with some labor, some sanding."

"Sanding?" I asked, looking over the impeccable forty-five foot, fiberglass boat he just stepped off of.

"Yes, sanding," he said, removing his sunglasses as he answered. "Do you know someone?"

"How many hours a week?" I asked right away, still curious.

"Oh, I don't know," he mused. "I guess I haven't thought that out." He looked out at the canal as he considered my question.

"How much an hour?" I followed up.

"Hmm," he responded, slowly, deep in thought. He brought his hand up and rubbed his chin as he contemplated the question. "Well, I guess it depends on what the person needs." He put his sunglasses back on and smiled. "We can figure those things as they go along, I suppose."

I wanted to know him. He seemed different from most people I had known, more at ease.

"So, sand what?" I asked, hoping for a specific answer.

"Well," he replied, looking me over again. "I'm going there now." I nodded and followed as he turned and started to walk down the dock.

The dock was narrow. I followed a step or two behind. Almost everyone we passed acknowledged the man. Towards the end of the dock, we took a left and walked up a small street into the sun. The street held art, and antique shops, a few restaurants and a splattering of historic houses people still lived in. The historic houses were identified with engraved plaques on the outside of their front doors. A block and a half up the street, he took a right into an alley between an art gallery and a residence. We walked through the shade between the buildings and came out behind the art gallery to an old boat covered in canvas. The tarped boat was on wooden stands and sat under an awning.

He walked over and pulled the canvas back from the side. "Nineteen forty-two Chris Craft, seventeen foot, mahogany top, just had the hull re-done," he said proudly. "I need to strip and sand the top and re-do the interior." He looked up from the boat and smiled. "They don't make them like this anymore."

"It looks rough," I said without thinking.

As he started to pull the tarps back, I moved to the other side to help. Once the tarps were removed, I saw that even unfinished, the boat was, as he implied, a work of art. He looked over the Chris Craft and ran his hands across the mahogany top. "I'm thinking sanding, taking off some hardware, and maybe taking the seats out to be re-upholstered," he said, answering my previous questions.

I looked over the boat and across the back of the property that overlooked the canal. "I don't really need the money, and I'm not much of a mechanic," I said.

He didn't say anything.

"I'd like to learn how to captain a boat," *What the hell, why not,* I thought.

"Well," he started, and then paused. "I go out every Sunday afternoon and usually mid-week to make sure she's running well. I suppose we could work something out." He walked over to me and extended his hand. "My name is David James," he said, "most call me Boat."

That was how I spent my summer. I worked with Boat sanding the old Chris Craft and learned how to captain a forty-five-foot boat.

Boat was warm and personal; he knew things, things I can't fully explain. I felt close to him, although he never directly answered a single question I asked. He responded with more depth and clarity through his stories and observations.

It was on the Bohemia River where I learned about Kin, the Tent Preacher, Caroline, and Annie. He told me the story of the Moon.

On a lazy summer day, he told me of Sal's exploits and about his writings, while we trolled down the Sassafras River.

We watched an Osprey build a nest as he spoke of the love that grew between Caroline and Kin.

On the Elk River, he told me of Peter, the Scotsman, and his early demise.

Under a low-hanging moon, coming in from the Chesapeake Bay, he spoke of Hope and Levon.

While sanding the mahogany top of the Chris Craft, he talked of Dr. Gerard, Kin and the kids, the vets they helped.

On the Northeast River, he told me of his own sin, his part in Jessie's unfortunate death. He talked of Kin's prison ministry and Sal's death.

That summer, I learned about faith, intent, and truth. I learned about the difficult moments of living an examined life, the confusion, the frustrations, and the loneliness. I learned the importance of being able to be held up by a single breeze and to continue on. I learned about connections, love, death, and tragedy.

I learned the difference between philosophical thinking and the conviction of practiced beliefs.

I learned the term practical spirituality.

I learned to see the light of waves.

I learned about redemption, being found, and salvation.

It's now late October.

The Chris Craft is finished and has been shipped out.

Boat and I stand on the dock as a cool autumn breeze pushes against us. He shakes my hand, turns and jumps onto his running boat. He's heading south.

I walk over to the tether ropes and toss them onto the boat. Instead of jumping on, as I have all summer, I stand on the dock alone.

Over the low grumble of the engine and churning water, I ask with a lump in my throat, "Will I see you again?"

He says nothing as the boat slowly drifts from the dock, gently rocking in the water.

After a few minutes, he smiles and speaks over the engine. "Probably not," he says with a sad smile. He scans the surrounding water.

The boat floats freely.

He looks back at me. His sad smile grows. "God speed," he shouts, gives me a last good look, nods his head, turns, and disappears into the cabin of the boat.

I look around, feeling shaken. The feeling leaves, and I find my own smile as I realize what he already knew. I couldn't ask any more of him if I wanted. He's shown me the commonalities, and the deep under-currents that transcend our commonplace thoughts and ideas. I better understand the things we all share, the things that matter.

Without telling me, he showed me I could find my own God.

We all can we should.

Maybe I got religion.

I watch as his boat drifts into the sunset.

Muted hues of red and purple that have escaped from behind the horizon find temporary spaces in the sky. Thin brushstrokes of gold and orange glow along the horizon and paint the undersides of low-hanging clouds.

The setting sun throws out a last beam of soft, glimmering light over the water and directly to me. The boat is now a silhouette against the sunset. I hate goodbyes.

As I watch his boat fade into the darkness, I feel the wind grow colder and stronger. I notice small waves begin to lap below the dock. Not ready to let go of the day, I zip up my jacket and sit cross-legged at the edge of the dock. A lone light buzzes and illuminates above me.

I scoot forward and let my legs hang over the edge of the dock. Leaning forward, I watch the water become still in between cycles of small waves. All the usual analogies of life - the calm and the turbulent - come to me as I watch.

Looking around, I notice a handful of scattered small stones on the dock near me. I'm sure the things he said were true, I think as I stretch to gather the stones in my reach.

I lean over the dock and drop one of the small stones into the calm water below. I watch as ripples slowly push out from the center. As the ripples fan out, a new cycle of waves come. I watch the waves until they slowly recede.

When the water again becomes still, I drop another stone into the water.

His words are still in my mind. Ripples within ripples are stories within stories. There is no beginning. This is where the ripples start, only to give themselves back to the water from whence they came.

www.ingramcontent.com/pod-product-compliance
Lightning Source LLC
Chambersburg PA
CBHW032121170626
46808CB00006B/2039